"Give me four weeks. Four weeks and I'll prove to you that I'm not the guy you think I am."

"You're kidding." She chuckled, then realized he wasn't laughing with her. "You can't seriously think us dating is a good idea."

"Why not? Are you worried that you'll get too attached and fall in love with me?"

In love? Not a chance. But she was already recklessly attracted to him, so she did have some concerns about letting him get too close. Unfortunately, she'd inherited that Sanchez competitive gene and she'd never been able to back down from a challenge.

"I'll give you two weeks." She took another bite of salad, hoping she wasn't going to regret this. "Two weeks will be long enough for you to realize that we're way too different to be together."

And not so long that they risked getting their hearts involved. Oh, who was she kidding? She was the only one at risk for that. But that didn't mean that she wasn't determined to prove him wrong.

"Three weeks," he countered. "That's long enough for me to convince you that we have a chance."

"Fine. Three weeks." She clinked his glass with her own in agreement. "If you can even last that long."

* * *

MONTANA MAVERICKS:
What Happened to Beatrix?

Dear Reader,

My aunt Lydia, affectionately known as Tia to me and my brothers, was first-generation Mexican American and an amazing cook. All of her recipes were in her head and if I wanted to learn how to make something, I had to sit in the kitchen with her and watch.

After she passed away, it felt odd making some of her favorite dishes and eventually, I worried that I'd forgotten the recipes. Recently, though, I've had more time to spend in the kitchen and have been experimenting again with the food from my childhood. My mom stopped by the other day and saw me making fresh salsa and asked why I was using a blender instead of dicing everything up.

Proud of myself for adhering to what I thought was a long-standing tradition, I replied, "Because that's the way Tia used to make it."

My mom laughed and said, "She only made it that way because Papa Sal hates onions and she had to blend them up so he wouldn't know they were there."

In *His Christmas Cinderella*, it was important to me that Camilla's Mexican American family had their own sense of tradition based on their unique experiences, especially when it came to food. In fact, Camilla's mom is loosely based on my *tia*, and Jordan's response to his first dinner with the Sanchez family is loosely based on my own husband's first dinner with the Duarte side of my family—lots of opinions and lots of food!

For more information on my other Harlequin Special Edition books chat with me on Twitter, @christyjeffries. You can also find me on Facebook and Instagram. I'd love to hear from you.

Enjoy,

Christy Jeffries

His Christmas Cinderella

CHRISTY JEFFRIES

HARLEQUIN
SPECIAL
EDITION

Special thanks and acknowledgment are given to Christy Jeffries for her contribution to the Montana Mavericks: What Happened to Beatrix? miniseries.

Recycling programs for this product may not exist in your area.

ISBN-13: 978-1-335-89488-5

His Christmas Cinderella

Christy Jeffries graduated from the University of California, Irvine, with a degree in criminology, and received her Juris Doctor from California Western School of Law. But drafting court documents and working in law enforcement was merely an apprenticeship for her current career in the dynamic field of mommyhood and romance writing. She lives in Southern California with her patient husband, two energetic sons and one sassy grandmother. Follow her online at christyjeffries.com.

Books by Christy Jeffries

Harlequin Special Edition

Sugar Falls, Idaho

A Marine for His Mom
Waking Up Wed
From Dare to Due Date
The Matchmaking Twins
The Makeover Prescription
A Family Under the Stars
The Firefighter's Christmas Reunion
The SEAL's Secret Daughter

American Heroes

A Proposal for the Officer

Montana Mavericks: The Lonelyhearts Ranch

The Maverick's Christmas to Remember

Visit the Author Profile page at Harlequin.com.

To Lydia Duarte Bustos. You were a strong and talented woman who could do it all and yet you never had a hair out of place. Nobody loved a party or family gathering as much as you. You were the biggest supporter of my mom's writing career, and I'm so sad that you never got to see me follow in her footsteps. I miss you, Tia!

Chapter One

In Jordan Taylor's experience, any party boasting this much wealth and this many business connections in one place—even if it was for a good cause—guaranteed that there would be plenty of beautiful women in attendance, as well. And the Denim and Diamonds gala his father and most recent stepmother were currently hosting promised all of the above.

Despite the theme, though, there were way more diamonds on display tonight than denim. Earlier today, a crew of workers had erected an enormous tent on the Taylor family's ranch for the occasion. Florists hauled in loads of arrangements and caterers set up food stations featuring only the finest cuts of Taylor beef while professional musicians tuned their instruments on the temporary stage above the dance floor. Judging by all the laughing, dancing and free-flowing champagne surrounding Jordan, Brittany Brandt Dubois, the professional party planner his father had hired, had more than earned her fees this evening.

Their friends and neighbors in Bronco Heights, Montana, might think the Taylors were simply raising money for programs to aid the families in need in nearby Bronco Valley. However, Jordan knew the truth. Cornelius Taylor III never missed an opportunity to showcase himself, his business, his ranch or his family. In that exact order.

Having dug his classic-cut tuxedo out of the back of his closet for the occasion, Jordan leaned against one of the tall blue-linen-draped cocktail tables. He lifted his glass of single malt Scotch in a mock toast to Cornelius and the much younger Jessica holding court in the center of the black tie crowd, then drained the smooth amber liquid and surveyed his options for some female companionship to otherwise distract him this evening.

Let's see. Who was here tonight?

Despite what the society columns and social media posts dubbed him, Jordan had *some* standards about who he dated. His gaze quickly passed from one young socialite to the next as he found reasons why they wouldn't interest him. Too young. Too old. Too boring. *Too married.* Too much drama.

Unfortunately, he usually had to leave Bronco if he wanted to meet someone he didn't already know. Or, rather, someone who didn't know *him.* Hell, he'd have to leave Montana for that.

Jordan glanced at the entrance just in time to see his sister, Daphne, hesitate before entering the party. Snagging two champagne flutes from a passing server, he cut a direct path toward her before she could change her mind and make a run for it.

"The prodigal daughter returns." He kissed Daphne on the cheek before handing her a crystal stem filled with liquid courage.

"Don't go killing the fatted calf on my behalf." Daphne quickly downed the first glass of bubbly, and Jordan handed her the second one. "You know I can't stand that sort of thing."

His chest expanded with defiance and he grinned. "That's why I spoke to the party planner ahead of time and arranged for a salad bar and a vegetarian station, right over there."

When a much younger Daphne first announced to her cattle ranching family that she was a vegetarian, Cornelius Taylor had rolled his eyes and suggested that his youngest daughter was simply going through a stage. When she opened her animal sanctuary instead of going to work in the family business, their father had accused Daphne of turning her back on her Taylor heritage and rejecting everything their ancestors stood for. Having three other uncles and a host of cousins who also took the family legacy seriously, his little sister had truly set herself up against a formidable wall of disapproval. Which made Jordan admire her courage all the more.

"Thanks." She offered a weak smile. "But I'm too nervous to eat anything. What did Dad say when you told him I was coming?"

Jordan knew better than to tell her what Cornelius had actually said. Even though their father was usually all bark and no bite, his harsh words would've only deepened the family rift. Their old man showed no signs of budging from his position of being the wronged party—at least in private. That was why Jordan had arranged for Daphne to attend the gala with so many people in attendance. "You know how Dad is with these public events. He'll be forced to lighten up. Or at least be polite so it doesn't cause a scene and bring shame to his upstanding position in the community."

"God forbid anyone think that the Taylors are anything less than perfect." Daphne lifted a corner of her mouth in a near smirk. "Luckily, Dad has the Crown Prince of Bronco Heights here tonight as his shining heir apparent."

Jordan playfully narrowed his eyes. "Keep it up and I'll take back that champagne I gave you."

Daphne finished off the second glass before wiggling her brows at him. "It's not like you didn't earn all those cutesy nicknames. What did that society blogger call you last week? 'He Who Will Not Be Tamed'?"

"So I like women." He crossed his arms on his chest. The narrow cut of the tailored tuxedo jacket uncomfortably bit into his biceps, the ridiculous formal garment proving to be just as restrictive as his family name. "Why is that such a newsworthy topic?"

"Because you like wo*men*. Plural, Jordan. It's never just one woman. I mean, it is for a week or two, but then you quickly move on to the next one before we even get a chance to learn her name. You know what you are? A serial dater."

"You say that like it's a bad thing. How do you expect me to settle down with the right lady if I haven't met her yet?"

"No need to settle down too soon, son." Their father clapped a beefy hand on Jordan's shoulder as he interrupted them. "I wish I would've sown my wild oats a little longer before I met your mother. Would've saved me a ton in alimony and attorney fees."

Jordan clenched his jaw to keep from outwardly cringing. Cornelius almost never mentioned his first wife. Or his second, for that matter. His doing so now wasn't likely due to any sentiment or nostalgia, though. Their father was trying to demonstrate a common bond between him and his oldest child, which would, in turn, imply how much Daphne *wasn't* like him. Luckily, his sister didn't rise to the bait.

"Daphne!" Jessica, their stepmother, rushed in and looped her arm through his sister's. "I'm so glad you could make it. There's someone I've been dying for you to meet."

As the two women walked away, Cornelius made a grumbling sound. "Did she ask you for a loan?"

"Who? Daphne?" Jordan felt a tic forming in his right temple. "No. Why would she need a loan?"

"For her Hippie Hearts save-the-animals place."

"Dad, you know damn right it's called Happy Hearts. And no, she is doing just fine financially."

"Well, you let me know if she's not. I may not approve of her most recent life choices, but us Taylors still need to always watch out for each other. How do we know her feed supplier or her hired hands aren't taking advantage of her goody goody nature?"

And so it began.

Jordan desperately needed another drink and a serious distraction from the lecture he knew his old man was about to deliver.

"Could you please get me another Macallan?" Jordan slipped a fifty-dollar bill to a passing server. "In fact, bring me the whole bottle," he added before his overprotective father started throwing around words like *exploitation*, *gold diggers*, and *access to family wealth*.

Jordan's eyes were about to glaze over from the familiar warnings when a vision in gold suddenly commanded his pupils to attention. A brunette in a shimmery sheath of sequins smiled at the person next to her. It might've been the deep V-cut of her dress that first caught Jordan's eye. However, it was those full red lips and dazzling smile that kicked Jordan right in the gut.

Her hair was slicked back into a long, dark ponytail, and her warm, golden skin was as smooth as polished topaz. Her big brown eyes sparkled as she laughed at whatever the person beside her said. Jordan felt a sudden pull to be the one who made her laugh like that.

"Who is that woman over there?" He interrupted his father's long-winded sermon.

"The one in the gold dress?" Cornelius

squinted, too vain to wear the glasses his op-
tometrist had prescribed. Clearly, though, the
old man still knew how to spot the most beautiful woman in the crowd. "That's Jose Balthazar's
daughter. I met her at that international cattle association event in Rio de Janeiro last year. Can't
think of her name off the top of my head, but
I had Jessica send an invitation to their North
American headquarters."

Now Jordan's interest was truly piqued. Beautiful, wealthy in her own right, and likely a smart
businesswoman if she took after her father. As
long as she was single, the lady in gold was
surely just what he needed to get his mind off
his own family drama. The server had impec-
cable timing, reappearing before the Taylor men
with the requested bottle and two crystal glasses
balanced perfectly on a silver tray.

"If you'll excuse me, I should probably go introduce myself to Miss Balthazar," Jordan told
his father. The empty glasses made a clinking
sound as he scooped them up in one hand and
grabbed the neck of the bottle in the other. "Keep
up with our foreign market interests and all that."

"Make sure she has a good time tonight." His
dad couldn't help but add some unsolicited advice before Jordan could make his getaway. "We
need the Balthazars and their shipping partners

to open a local office if we want to keep our exporting costs down."

The last thing on Jordan's mind right that second, though, was business.

According to the storybooks, Cinderella had gone to the ball purely out of curiosity. To see how the other half lived. Camilla Sanchez, on the other hand, was at this particular ball tonight for one purpose only. To network with potential investors for the restaurant she'd been carefully planning for the past six years.

Not that the Denim and Diamonds gala was an actual ball. It was a fundraiser. Albeit a very lavish fundraiser with very wealthy guests who were often considered the royalty of Montana. Camilla certainly wasn't anyone's idea of royalty.

The city of Bronco was made up of two areas. There was Bronco Heights, where the wealthy cattle barons and affluent landowners rubbed elbows at parties like this, displaying their vast riches and sitting on their powerful thrones.

Then there was Bronco Valley, where Camilla lived.

As excited as she'd been when her boss and his wife first invited her to attend with them tonight and sit at their table, it had taken less than an hour for Camilla to feel out of place and overwhelmed. Of course, it didn't help that the bouncer at the entrance had radioed something to one of the other security guards right as he was checking her invitation. Any second now, she expected to get ousted as some sort of imposter who wasn't actually there to write a hefty donation check or bid on the fancy silent auction items that she couldn't possibly afford. She was the denim compared to everyone else's diamonds.

Smiling politely at Melanie Driscoll, her former manager, Camilla checked the time only to see a row of faux gold bangle bracelets where her watch normally sat. Ugh. Had Cinderella ever wanted to dash out of her ball a few hours early?

While Camilla's borrowed ball gown wouldn't vanish at the stroke of midnight, it was way pricier than what she could afford on her waitress salary. It was also way more revealing than anything she was accustomed to wearing. Looking down, Camilla sucked in a breath and subtly tried to adjust the plunging neckline of her dress. Before she could exhale and lift her head, she noticed the black satin lapels of a tuxedo jacket directly before her.

"Let me welcome you to the Taylor Ranch." The very smooth and very masculine voice made her gulp before she could even lift her gaze.

Jordan Taylor needed no introduction. Not

only had she gone to the same high school as him—she'd been several years behind the legendary homecoming king and star wide receiver who still held the school record for most touchdown receptions—Camilla often saw his name and picture in social media posts and local newspaper articles. In fact, anyone who'd lived in Montana the past six months knew who the illustrious Taylors were. Jordan's most newsworthy nicknames were The Crown Prince of Bronco Heights, Bronco Heights' Most Eligible Rancher, and He Who Will Not Be Tamed.

And he was welcoming her to his home and pouring her a glass of…Scotch? Did she even drink Scotch? Well, if she wanted to impress him with her restaurant and possibly bar knowledge, she might as well start now. She accepted one of the two glasses he'd so deftly balanced in his hands as he'd poured straight from a bottle she recognized as very expensive top-shelf liquor.

Should she introduce herself? That might be weird since he hadn't offered his own name. Not that he needed to. Smiling to calm her fluttering nerves, she nodded at his bottle service skills. "Clearly, you have experience pouring drinks."

His deep grin revealed a wealth of charm and matching dimples in each cheek. A rich boy who was used to getting whatever he wanted. "I did my share of bartending back in college."

"Oh, really?" Camilla took a small sip of the amber liquid in an effort to hide her curiosity. She was here to meet potential investors, after all. If he had experience in the service industry, he might be interested in her ideas about opening her restaurant. "Was it at a chain restaurant or a dive bar or—"

His soft chuckle cut her off. "No, not professionally or anything like that. I usually only manned the bar at our fraternity parties. I can mix a mean sangria, though."

Of course the heir to the Taylor fortune hadn't actually had to work for a living in college. Camilla took another sip and felt both the alcohol and the disappointment burn down her throat. Yet she'd had enough experience in the service industry that she knew how to paste on her own charming smile. "I'm sure all those sorority sisters loved your sangria."

"Just between me and you…" He leaned in closer, and Camilla felt a heat spread through her. It must be the Scotch. "Being the bartender was actually my trick to *avoid* the sorority girls. Or at least avoiding them on the dance floor."

The band's lead singer directed everyone to go check out the silent auction items before launching into the appropriately titled Pink Floyd classic "Money."

As partygoers wandered away from the dance

floor to hopefully spend their cash on things they didn't need, Jordan surprised her by asking, "How's your father?"

"My father?" How did Jordan Taylor know Camilla's father? Aaron Sanchez had worked at the only post office in Bronco for the past thirty or so years. But Jordan didn't look like the type of guy who trekked into town every day to pick up his own mail. He probably had a slew of employees who did that for him. "He's fine?"

"I heard he had surgery last month," he said, and Camilla tried not to stare at the tan column of his neck as he tilted his head back and swallowed the contents of his glass. "My assistant sent something. A wine basket, I believe."

"A wine basket?" Camilla repeated, then shook her head to clear it. A few neighbors had dropped off casseroles, but she was pretty sure she would've remembered if her dad had gotten a wine basket after his bunion surgery. Especially one from the Taylors.

"Speaking of fathers," Jordan continued. "I believe my dad mentioned something about you and your family expanding your business ventures to Bronco Heights."

Camilla's hand flew to her chest. How did he already know that? Did they vet all the guests ahead of time? And expanding their business ventures was a lofty way to put it. Her mom

managed a somewhat upscale beauty salon, but
that was pretty much the extent of the Sanchezes'
global enterprises. She cleared her throat. "Well,
the restaurant I'm planning to open is more of
my venture than my family's. I mean, obviously,
they'll support me in any way they can, but I'm
actually looking for outside investors."

As soon as she said the words *outside investors*, Jordan's eyes veered away from her as
though he'd caught a glance of something more
interesting. Great. She was already boring him.
At least he was polite enough to ask, "What kind
of restaurant?"

"Well, Mexican food primarily, but not Tex
Mex. I've got a ton of my grandmother's old
recipes, although I'm not actually a trained chef.
I'd have to hire someone to run the kitchen, but
I have a ton of experience with running everything else in a restaurant." Camilla had prac-
ticed the sales pitch several times in the mirror
before coming tonight. However, now that she
was standing in front of one of the wealthiest—
and best-looking—men in Montana, she was getting it all wrong.

She exhaled. It wasn't as though Jordan was
particularly paying attention to her right that second anyhow. His gaze seemed to be focused on
a very pretty and very pregnant woman on the
other side of the dance floor.

"Did you need to go talk to her?" Camilla offered the same pleasant smile she would use when asking a customer if she could bring him the check.

"Uh, no." Jordan's head whipped back in Camilla's direction. "Erica is friends with my sister and I was just thinking that Daphne would be happy to see a familiar face."

"Oh, so she's a family friend?" Camilla asked, knowing that it really wasn't any of her business if he was staring at every single woman at the gala. A guy like Jordan Taylor didn't get a nickname like Rancher Most Wanted because he could focus all his attention on only one female. He oozed charm and even if she wasn't already familiar with his reputation, Camilla had dated enough good-looking guys to know a player when she met one.

"Well, our families go way back," he replied. Then he surprised her by admitting, "Erica and I actually went out on a few dates one summer when I was home from college, mostly to appease our parents. She moved back to Bronco recently, and even though I've seen her a handful of times since then, it's still weird seeing kids I grew up with come back to town as grown-up adults with these totally different lives."

His sentimental words settled deep into Camilla's chest, and something about Jordan's eyes made her momentarily doubt all the rumors she'd ever heard about him. But only momentarily.

"I get that." She nodded. "Every time one of my friends gets married or has a baby, I feel as though I'm standing still while everyone else is moving ahead."

"Exactly!" Jordan lifted the bottle of Scotch as though in a mock salute. "If you're not settled down and starting a family by age thirty, society begins to think there's something wrong with you."

Her eyes traced down his broad shoulders and lean waist in that custom-made tuxedo.

"I seriously doubt that anybody thinks there is something wrong with you." As soon as the words left her mouth, Camilla sucked in a breath and prayed he hadn't heard her over the opening strains of the band's next song.

Unfortunately, his knowing smile told her otherwise. "Coming from the most beautiful woman in the room tonight, I'll defer to your judgment on the subject."

A flush of heat stole up her neck and face. Her mother had insisted on doing Camilla's hair and makeup before the party, and now she hoped the pricey bronzer on her cheeks hid her embarrassment. "Oh, I don't know if it's *my* expertise that you'd want. I'm afraid I'm in the same boat as you when it comes to settling down. It seems like there's so much to do before I can even think about going along that same path as everyone else."

He lifted his dark eyebrows and Camilla was about to artfully bring the conversation back to her restaurant. But before she could bring up potential investors again, he asked her a question. "You know this song?"

Camilla was surprised the band had moved on from 1980s hits and was now covering a Bruno Mars song, yet her hips naturally moved along to the thrumming hip-hop beat. "It's one of my favorites."

"Mine, too." He downed the rest of his drink before gesturing toward the parquet floor that must've cost thousands of dollars to rent in order to cover the expanse of grass inside the heated tent. "Let's go out there and show everyone that we've got a lot of living left to do before we settle down."

The fast-paced song meant that no touching was required, but that didn't stop Camilla's body from reacting to the way Jordan moved. Or to the way he watched her as she threw back her shoulders, dipped her knees and rolled her hips to the beat. It was as though someone had tied a string around both of their waists, connecting them by a thin thread that they couldn't break.

A second song started, this one by Beyoncé,

and even more people poured onto the dance floor. The chemistry between her and Jordan must've been obvious to everyone else, because even with the crowd jockeying for position around them, the other partygoers gave them their space. The heart-pounding music threatened to take over her body and her judgment, and Camilla had to keep dancing just to keep from drowning in his chocolate-brown eyes. The very same eyes that made her feel as if she were the only woman here with him.

Despite knowing his reputation, by the third song, she finally succumbed to the thrill that Bronco Heights' most eligible bachelor had chosen *her* as his dance partner. At some point, Jordan had shrugged out of his jacket and Camilla had to make a concerted effort to keep her focus above his chest. Speaking of chests, she needed to be sure that the double-sided tape keeping her plunging neckline in place didn't slip and cause a wardrobe malfunction.

Earlier in the day, she'd expressed that same concern to her sister Sofia, a stylist at a fashionable boutique in Bronco Heights who had loaned her the ball gown. Sofia had assured her that everyone at the gala would be standing around networking and complimenting each other on their substantial donations to charity. Nobody would be hopping around on the dance floor like a bunch of teenagers at their high school prom. Camilla couldn't wait to tell her little sister how wrong she'd been.

She attempted a casual dance move that simultaneously allowed her to adjust the narrow strips of sequined fabric covering her breasts, yet she only succeeded in drawing Jordan's eyes to that exact spot. When the tempo quickly changed to a slow song, it seemed only natural for him to pull her into his arms.

The warm fabric of his starched white dress shirt pressed against Camilla's flushed skin and she slid her own arms around his neck, her face turning toward the sleekly knotted black tie at his throat. Lord help her, she thought as she inhaled the musky scent of cedar wood and damp skin. The man smelled even better than he danced.

Her heart pulsed behind her rib cage as Jordan's fingers carelessly traced circles along her lower spine. Or maybe his fingers weren't careless at all, but very, *very* methodical. *Don't think about how perfectly you fit against him*, she commanded herself. *Just enjoy the moment.* When was the last time she'd been out dancing? Her cousin Bianca's wedding, maybe? Surely, way before she'd picked up those extra waitressing shifts. Usually, her already exhausted feet

were much too tired to do more than hold her upright in a steamy shower at the end of a long day.

"Hey, Camilla!" DJ Traub, the owner of DJ's
Deluxe, interrupted her romantic thoughts. Her
boss had maneuvered his wife beside them on
the dance floor. "Have you mentioned your restaurant idea to Jordan yet?"

The man's reminder was as subtle as a
dropped tray of dishes. She was here to find investors, not to be seduced by the town's most
infamous bachelor.

Jordan pulled back, but only slightly, keeping his gaze locked on her as he spoke to the
other man. "Camilla and I spoke briefly about
it. Although we haven't negotiated whether
Taylor Beef will be one of her main suppliers."
He looked into her upturned face. "Maybe we
should go sample some of the product?"

A ripple of anticipation zipped through her.
Was he serious? She was still in the early stages
of finding investors, yet Jordan was already
miles ahead of her, talking about food suppliers. Sure, he might be a savvy businessman and
probably easily navigated his way through many
deals. But would he really be laying on this much
charm to negotiate a deal if he didn't believe in
her restaurant?

Trying to get her head back in the game, Camilla allowed him to lead her to one of the food

stations, where they were serving bite-sized beef Wellington pastries and prime rib sliders. The scent of the garlicky horseradish sauce helped clear her sinuses and her mind.

"Sounds like you're not going to have any problem getting your restaurant up and running if you've already got DJ Traub talking about it." Jordan handed her a small appetizer plate and his fingers brushed against hers.

That anticipatory thrill shot through Camilla again, but this time it wasn't just because of Jordan's nearness. DJ wasn't only her boss, he was one of the best known restaurateurs in Montana. He'd known that by bringing Camilla to this fundraiser as his guest, he was all but assuring the public of his faith in her. Now it was time for her to do her part and seal the deal.

Camilla took a deep breath. "You know, I put together a financial proposal if you'd be interested in reviewing it."

"I'd love to review it." Jordan smiled again and Camilla's legs turned to jelly. "Just as long as we're clear that I'd be looking at it as a *friend*, not as an investor."

"Oh." Camilla tightened her spine to keep her shoulders from sagging with disappointment.

Jordan put a finger under her chin, forcing her to meet his direct stare. "Camilla, I never mix business with pleasure. If we were to work together, then we couldn't dance together like that again. And I really, *really* enjoy dancing with you."

"Thank you." One of her eyebrows lifted slightly. "I think."

"But I can introduce you to one of my uncles. His daughter did a semester abroad in Mexico City a few years ago and is still talking about the lack of good authentic food in Bronco." Jordan put two sliders on her plate, added several savory puffed pastries, then loaded them both down with skewers of tender marinated steak and a yogurt cucumber dipping sauce. "Let's grab another drink and maybe one or two more dances, and then we can go find my Uncle Thaddeus and maybe talk to a couple of my business associates."

Camilla followed him as he cut a path to one of the bars set up on the perimeter of the massive tent. Part of her had been hoping that having Jordan investing in her restaurant would be a quick and easy solution. The other part of her was trying to tell her giddy nerves that he was right and there was no way they could be business partners considering how her body reacted to his on the dance floor. Besides, she'd known that she wasn't going to hook an investor at her very first event. She was supposed to be meeting people and mingling tonight, networking and forming her own connections.

This time, instead of offering her a bottle of Scotch, Jordan stood back while she ordered a spicy jalapeno mojito from the bartender. They ate, they laughed and they tried each other's drinks. Then they ate a little more. It was almost easier being around Jordan now that Camilla didn't have to impress him—at least not in the business sense.

The only awkward moment came when Cornelius Taylor took the microphone to announce how much money they'd raised so far tonight. It was an obscene amount that none of the local community fundraisers she'd volunteered for ever brought in. She wanted to ask Jordan which local charities would be getting the proceeds from tonight, but she'd noticed the firm set of his jaw while his father was on stage and decided not to dip her toe into those tense waters.

When a country-and-Western song came on afterward, Jordan quickly pulled her onto the dance floor to teach her how to two-step. "Cha Cha Slide" came on next, and it was her turn to teach him how to do a line dance. His feet went to the left and his arms went to the right, and when it came time to hop five times, Camilla had never laughed so hard in her life.

Another slow song started and when he pulled

her close a second time, Camilla realized that she never wanted tonight to end. As soon as the thought popped into her mind, another couple bumped into them.

It was Erica Abernathy Dalton, her face completely drained of color. "I think I'm going to have a baby."

Chapter Two

Camilla felt Jordan's hand squeeze her waist before he dropped his arm. "I'm going to call an ambulance. Would you mind staying with them?"

"Of course," she replied, sliding closer to Erica and helping the pregnant woman's husband lead her off the dance floor.

Camilla had never actually witnessed a birth—not even on an online video. She prayed that tonight wasn't yet another first for her. Camilla hadn't been exaggerating when she'd told Jordan that she'd had no desire to follow in any of her friends' footsteps and get married or have

kids anytime soon. This all looked way too pain-
ful and complicated.

"Should you sit down?" she asked Erica,
whose mouth was in a perfect circle and puff-
ing out short bursts of air.

"No. The contraction is easing up now."
Erica whistled air through gritted teeth. Erica's
husband—Camilla thought she'd heard someone call him Morgan—asked people to clear out
of the way so they could get through to the tent
opening.

Several other people crowded around the la-
boring woman, wanting to offer any help they
could. The band stopped playing and more and
more guests became curious about what was
going on.

"The ambulance is on its way." Jordan returned with his cell phone pressed against his
ear. "How far apart are the contractions?"

Erica was now seated on one of the chairs
and as more bystanders arrived, Camilla was
slowly edged out of the way. And really, it was
just as well. She didn't know these people and
she certainly didn't know a thing about deliver-
ing babies. There wasn't anything she could do
but get in the way.

Jordan, though, had sprung into action, direct-
ing both the staff and the guests. First he ordered
people to give Erica space. Then he told some

random guy in a bright blue tuxedo to fetch a glass of water before instructing the security guards to ensure the long driveway was cleared for the ambulance's arrival. His take-charge attitude was quite the reversal of his earlier laid-back mood, and Camilla almost wanted to stay just so she could watch him in action.

Really, though, there was no point in her staying. Not only would Jordan be preoccupied for the rest of the night, it wasn't as though Camilla could walk up and introduce herself to Jordan's Uncle Thaddeus or any of the Taylor cousins to discuss her business model while one of the guests was currently in labor. Besides, Camilla had already gotten what she came for—some buzzing interest about her up-and-coming restaurant and even some tips about possible investors.

It was probably best to leave now with the success of the evening still glowing inside her. Camilla grabbed her faux fur stole and purse from her assigned table, and had just handed her ticket to the valet parking attendant when Jordan caught up with her.

"Camilla, wait!" Jordan was still in his white dress shirt, but the tie was undone and his sleeves were rolled up. "I saw you walking out and didn't want you leaving without saying goodbye."

"Oh, don't worry about it. I didn't want to be

in the way in there and figured everyone would be leaving soon anyway."

"I'd offer to drive you, but I should probably stay here until the ambulance arrives." Jordan craned his neck to look toward the paved private road leading to his family's ranch house. Lines of concern marred his forehead, his expression the exact opposite of the confident charmer she'd met earlier this evening. "I don't know why it's taking so long."

Camilla suppressed a chuckle. Of course Jordan wasn't used to waiting for anything. What he didn't realize, though, was that the Bronco City Council had approved a new fire station to be built in the wealthier area of the Heights, despite the fact that the majority of residents lived in the Valley. So the ambulances were usually called down the hill to assist with the regular folks, making the EMTs less likely to be on standby for the citizens of the Heights. But the poor guy was nervously rocking back and forth in his fancy black cowboy boots, so she didn't have the heart to get into a discussion about the disparities in their town's designation of civic resources.

"Like I said, please don't worry about it." Her smile wasn't forced when she added, "I had a lot of fun tonight."

"Good." Jordan's shoulders relaxed before he

reached out and traced a finger along her bare arm. "You have no idea how much better my evening got once I finally met you."

She wanted to tell him that she bet he said that to all the girls. But those dark brown eyes of his were so focused and seemed so entirely serious that Camilla found herself at a complete loss of words.

"Before I saw you, I was counting the minutes until I could leave." He took a step closer and Camilla felt a shiver travel down her back. His voice lowered. "As soon as I started talking to you, though, the night became almost magical."

She tilted her face to look up at him just before he lowered his lips to hers, brushing them ever so slightly against her open mouth. Camilla wasn't entirely sure the contact would count as a kiss, yet the tingling sensation spreading through her suggested it was even more intimate than anything she'd ever experienced. At least in public.

In fact, she almost lifted on tiptoe to try the kiss again, but a siren sounded in the distance. Several more partygoers spilled out of the tent, and Camilla jumped back. Jordan looked over his shoulder before he squeezed her hand. "I hope I can see you again, Miss Balthazar."

Camilla's heart immediately dropped into the pit of her stomach and the red warning lights flashing all around her weren't just from the approaching emergency responders.

Who in the world was Miss Balthazar? Had he mistaken her for someone else?

Her mind tried to race through all their earlier conversations to recall if either one of them had ever mentioned her last name. But her brain and her blood felt as though they were frozen. Luckily, the parking attendant pulled her car along the other side of the recently arrived ambulance. She needed to get out of here before he found out she wasn't who he thought she was.

"Thank you again for a lovely evening," she called out before rushing off into the night. Cinderella herself hadn't made such a dramatic exit.

At least Camilla hadn't left so much as a glass slipper behind.

Jordan sat in his office, scrolling through last night's RSVP list on his laptop.

"It'd be quicker if you just tell me what, or *who*, you're looking for and I find her myself." Mac, his personal assistant, came around to his side of the desk.

Jordan didn't lift his eyes from the digital spreadsheet. "Why are you assuming it's a female I'm looking for?"

"When are you *not* in search of a female?" Mac leaned in closer, squinting despite the fact that her smudged spectacles were perched on top of her Bronco Valley Little League ball cap. Jordan's own grandfather had hired the woman fresh out of secretarial school back in the fifties, and the older woman liked to remind Jordan that she'd been an employee of Taylor Beef longer than any of them. "Besides, you never ask me to forward you emails from Little Cornelius's public relations team. Something's up."

"You know, Mac, I think you're the only person alive who can still get away with calling my old man Little Cornelius."

"That's because I used to change his diapers just like I did yours," Mac easily replied. "It's the same reason why I can get people around this place to provide me party lists with no questions asked."

Jordan agreed. The fewer people who knew about his little extracurricular search, the better. That included Mac. "Don't you have a batting lineup or something you need to work on right now?"

"Nope." Mac tugged on the faded red jersey with Senior Swingers stitched across the front. His assistant was well past eighty years old and didn't really assist Jordan so much as act as a gatekeeper from keeping Cornelius and some of the other members of the board of directors from bugging Jordan while he worked. In exchange for her loyalty and dedication, he didn't complain about the fact that Mac used her desk outside of his office as her coaching headquarters for the two Little League and three year-round recreational softball teams she managed. "Not when my boy is planning to make some calls to the bullpen to send another rookie to the pitching mound."

"Can you please stop comparing my dating life to a sporting event?" Jordan's eye caught on the letter C on his screen, but the name beside it was Carmichael, not Camilla.

"Well, if the cleat fits…" Mac rested a bony elbow on Jordan's shoulder. She clearly wasn't leaving his office anytime soon.

"I'm trying to get a phone number for Camilla Balthazar." He released a heavy breath. "But I'm not seeing her on the RSVP list. In fact, I'm not seeing anyone named Camilla."

"There's an Alexis Balthazar." Mac pointed out the same thing Jordan's eye kept coming back to. He'd never really asked the woman her name last night, but DJ Traub had referred to her as Camilla. Maybe DJ had gotten the name wrong, but she'd been too polite to correct him. Jordan racked his brain trying to remember if he'd called her by the wrong name, as well.

"I think this number beside her name is for the North American headquarters." Jordan kept his fingers from reaching for his phone. The best way to avoid Mac's sports-announcer-type commentary was to ask her to do her actual job. "Will you see if you can track down a direct phone line for Alexis?"

"No can do, Sport." Mac stood up and made a motion as though she was swinging a bat. "You know what my training is like during the off-season. I've gotta get to the indoor cages before the Bronco Bombers get there and take all the fast pitch machines."

Jordan held back his knowing grin as the woman who was more like a grandmother to him took off for yet another practice. Then he shut his office door before dialing the number.

After being transferred to three different extensions and repeating the name "Jordan Taylor from Taylor Beef" at least five times, he finally reached Alexis Balthazar's assistant, who told him that the corporate jet was grounded last night in Brussels unexpectedly. The man added that Miss Balthazar was sorry she'd missed the Denim and Diamonds gala and would be sending a sizable donation when she returned to the States.

Jordan stared at the phone for several seconds after he hung up. He typed the name Alexis Balthazar into his internet search engine, and the image that popped up on his screen was a long-haired brunette, but the eye color and the cheekbones and the smile were all wrong. This definitely was not the same woman from last night.

Did Jose have another daughter? He scanned the company's website for a list of employees, but didn't see anyone named Camilla. Jordan tried several more internet searches before his cell phone vibrated with a text notification from Daphne.

Erica had a GIRL! They named her Josie after her Grandpa Josiah. Isn't that sweet? Mom and baby are both doing well.

Jordan made a mental note to send a card or something to the hospital when a second text bubble appeared from Daphne. Glad last night was a success for someone.

Damn. He'd been so focused on Camilla last night that he hadn't even checked in with his sister. Jordan quickly pressed the green phone icon to call Daphne, who picked up on the second ring.

"I take it things didn't go well between you and the old man last night?" he asked.

"It was a total disaster. Dad told me that it was never too late to apologize and admit that the animal sanctuary was a mistake. I told him not to hold his breath."

"Good for you."

"Yeah. Good for me. Except he walked away and pretty much froze me out for the rest of the night. It was so uncomfortable. At one point, we were standing next to each other at the bar and Daniel Dubois asked how things were going and Dad pretended like I wasn't even there."

"Sounds like something he'd do." Jordan put the phone on speaker and kept clicking on the keys on his laptop. He felt bad for Daphne, but they both knew how Cornelius was. He loved his children, even if he had the most frustrating way of expressing it. This kind of passive aggressive behavior was nothing new and eventually the old man would come around. "Dad can't stand not getting his way so he'll pretend the problem doesn't even exist. Not that you're a problem. It's just in his mind…you know?"

"Oh, I know all right." Daphne snorted. "If you're not with him, you're against him and all that. What's that clicking sound? Are you typing while you're talking to me?"

"Sort of. I'm trying to find someone who was at the party last night. Do you remember Jose Balthazar?"

"Not really. But I remember his daughter.

Alexis and I went to that all girls' camp together during our high school winter breaks."

"Did he have any other daughters? There was a woman last night at the party named Camilla and—"

"The brunette in the gold sequined gown?" Daphne interrupted.

"Yes!" His pulse sped up. "Did you talk to her?"

"Jordan, I don't think anyone besides you had a chance to talk with her. With the way you two were moving on the dance floor, I don't think anyone wanted to come between you."

"Aha! So I wasn't just imagining that we had a connection." Jordan almost pumped his fist in triumph. Instead, he settled for doing a full one-eighty spin in his custom leather desk chair.

"C'mon, Jor. Half the female population of Montana thinks they have a connection with you."

"But this was different. This time, *I* was the one feeling the connection."

Jordan could almost see Daphne rolling her eyes before she said, "Well, I can't help you. I have no idea who she was."

"Dad told me it was Jose Balthazar's daughter."

"Nope. Alexis is the only girl in that family as far as I know. Besides, you know how bad Dad's eyes are when he refuses to wear his glasses."

Crap. Jordan had forgotten about that part.

"So how do I find her?" he asked his sister.

"You don't. If a woman wants to be found, she'll find you first."

"But I'm not even sure of her real name. Maybe you could ask some of your friends…"

"You know who you sound like right now?" Daphne asked, but didn't wait for an answer. "Dad."

"That's hitting below the belt," he replied, not really joking.

"It's true. Once you get your mind set on something, you can't let it go."

Jordan felt his nostrils expand as he sucked in a calming breath. He was used to the nicknames and the teasing and the constant references to his dating history. But Jordan had worked his entire life to be the opposite of his father. To not take things so seriously or care what people thought about him. To not get too attached to anyone, especially women who might leave.

"Listen, I gotta get going," he said, wanting to end the call as politely as possible. He also didn't want his sister to realize how much her comparison had bothered him. She was already dealing with enough when it came to their family.

"So you can get back to the search for your missing Cinderella?"

"No, so that I can order something to be delivered to Erica at the hospital," he said, which wasn't a total lie. Although as soon as he placed the order online, he had every intention of resuming his search for the woman who'd fled the ball right before the stroke of midnight.

Not that his conversation with his sister had made him feel like any sort of Prince Charming. Far from it, in fact.

After Daphne said goodbye, he tried to remind himself that his sister was actually annoyed at their father, not Jordan. However, her expressing her doubt about his intentions still stung. Especially because what he'd experienced last night was different. Camilla was special.

If Camilla was, in fact, her real name.

Jordan drummed his fingers beside the computer mouse. His sister's words bounced around in his head. *If a woman wants to be found, she'll find you first.* Most of the women he'd ever dated, and even a few he hadn't dated, had always sought him out or made it more than clear that they were available if he were to ask them out. But Jordan had a feeling Camilla wasn't most women.

He returned his attention to his laptop and clicked on his stepmother's social media page to see if photos from the night before had already been uploaded. Sure enough, there were several... dozen. In the very last one, he was finally able to zoom in on a woman in a gold sequined gown sitting at a table with DJ Traub and his wife.

Jordan picked up his phone to call DJ, but had second thoughts. They were really more acquaintances than anything else. DJ's Deluxe did some business with Taylor Beef, keeping the local restaurant well stocked with their best cuts of meat, but that was his Uncle Lester's account. He couldn't just randomly call the man out of the blue and ask about the woman who'd been sitting at his table.

Instead, Jordan typed DJ's name in the search field on his social media tab and quickly found the page for the popular restaurant in Bronco Heights. Most of the images were of the food and the decor, but in the grand opening crowd, he thought he saw someone who might be Camilla.

An electrical current raced through him now that he'd found a clue about the woman from last night. Grabbing his car keys, he strode down the hall and out the building. He suddenly had an unexplainable craving for a porterhouse and another glass of Macallan.

Camilla's arm was already buckling under the weight of the tray holding several sizzling cast iron plates artfully displaying tonight's special—peppercorn-encrusted filet mignon in a mushroom and red wine reduction sauce, potatoes au gratin and steamed asparagus with an herbed lemon zest.

She was exhausted and deflated and couldn't wait to get off work and go climb into her bed. After Jordan had called her by the wrong name last night, she'd tossed and turned, thinking about how the only reason he'd even talked to her was that he'd thought she was someone else. She'd gotten maybe two hours of sleep this morning before having to be up for her Managerial Economics class at eight sharp. Thank God for online classes—at least she could watch the lecture in her pajamas with her hair in a messy bun and last night's leftover mascara still stuck to her lashes.

After finishing her paper on regression analysis in today's service industry, she'd hoped to get a little nap in before her afternoon shift at DJ's Deluxe. Instead, her sister asked her to drop off the borrowed dress at the dry cleaners. Then her dad needed a ride to his doctor's appointment because he wasn't supposed to be driving yet postsurgery, and her mom couldn't take him because Mrs. Waters had shown up at the salon after trying to do another home perm. The rest of Camilla's afternoon had been an entire blur.

But through it all, she kept moving, which kept her from having to mentally relive the embarrassing mix-up last night. Serving at a restaurant was a comforting routine to her. She delivered the plates to one table, dropped off the check at a second table, and was in the middle of taking a drink order from a third when she realized someone sitting at the bar was watching her.

Jordan Taylor.

Camilla froze with her pen hovering over the pad. Even if she'd wanted to dive for cover under the white-linen-draped table, her body refused to move. Why was he here? She hadn't even had time to think about the man since she'd awoken this morning. And that was a good thing. Or at least it had been.

"What kind of craft beers do you have on tap?" a customer asked, jarring her back to the real world. She was no longer at the Denim and Diamonds gala. She had a living to earn.

Despite the fact that Camilla had both the wine and beer lists memorized, she didn't trust herself not to stutter or lose focus. Instead, she told the customer, "I'll go get you a menu. Be right back."

Maybe that had been the wrong stall tactic, she realized, as she was now forced to walk toward the bar to retrieve the printed parchment tucked into a leather folder. Jordan's mouth split into that boyishly charming grin as she approached.

"Hey," he said, showcasing those knee-wobbling dimples in his cheeks.

"What are you doing here?" she asked.

"I thought about playing it cool and saying I came in for an after-work drink and a perfectly cooked ribeye. But the truth is that I was hoping to see you again."

"Why?"

"Because I've been trying to find you all day."

She refused to let her heart do a repeat of last night. "Were you looking for me? Or were you looking for Miss Balthazar?"

"Yeah, I'm really sorry for that mix-up. My father was the one who told me you were the daughter of one of our business associates. The old man is too vain to admit that he needs glasses and I was too mesmerized by you to even ask for confirmation." He formally stuck out his hand as though he hadn't just kissed her on the lips last night. Or sort of kissed her. "I'm Jordan Taylor, by the way."

"Yes, I know," she replied. The tray was still tucked under her arm, so she had an excuse to decline the handshake. But she didn't want to seem bitter. Or affected by his presence either way. She set the tray on the bar and took his offered hand. Ignoring the riptide of electricity that sailed through her skin, she added, "If you'll excuse me, I need to get going."

"Wait," he said before she could turn around. "Can I maybe buy you a drink? We could sit down and talk."

"Listen, I know you thought I was someone else last night. But I'm a waitress, not a socialite at one of your parties." She looked pointedly around at the almost full tables in the expensive restaurant tastefully decorated to accentuate its rustic origins. Then she gestured to her uniform of a white blouse, black slacks and a long black waist apron. "I'm at work."

"Right." He nodded. She had a feeling he wasn't used to being told no, even if it was for a good reason—such as not losing her job. "Then can I get your number so that I can call you later?"

"Here's the thing, Jordan. I had a great time last night. And I appreciate you coming in and making the attempt. I'm flattered. However, we all know how this will turn out."

"How *what* will turn out?"

"This." She gestured between the two of them. "Us. It might be a fun diversion for a few hours, or maybe even a few days. And if I wasn't working full-time *and* in the middle of my MBA program *and* trying to open my own restaurant, then maybe I wouldn't mind a little…distraction." She caught herself before she used the words *booty call*.

"You know…" He tilted his head and dropped his eyes to the name tag on her white uniform shirt. "You still haven't told me your full name."

If this guy was some sort of stalker who refused to take no for an answer, she certainly wasn't going to make it any easier for him. "Why do you need it?"

"Because I've been talking to a few people who may be interested in investing in your restaurant."

She narrowed her eyes. So maybe Jordan wasn't a full-blown stalker. Especially considering the fact that his reputation would suggest he was way more likely to be the one being stalked. Still. There was no reason to completely throw caution to the wind and let him think that she had any interest in him other than professional.

"It's Camilla Sanchez. If one of your contacts wants to get in touch with me, I would suggest they do so when it's not during the dinner rush."

"Fair enough," he said, that satisfied grin spreading across his way too handsome face.

Determined to maintain the upper hand, Camilla returned to her waiting customers, only to realize that she'd completely forgotten the beer list. It took her another hour to get back into the swing of things. By eight-thirty, most of her tables had cleared out and only the customers who couldn't book earlier reservations remained.

When she finally folded her apron and collected her tips, it was nine o'clock.

And Jordan Taylor was waiting by the hostess desk for her.

Chapter Three

"You don't give up easily, do you?" Camilla asked Jordan.

"Well you *did* say to come back when you weren't working."

"No. I said one of those potential investors you were talking about could talk to me when I wasn't working. And I specifically remember you saying last night that you had no plans to invest in my restaurant because, what was the tired cliché you used?" She tapped her chin thoughtfully as if she didn't already have it seared in her brain. "You don't mix business with pleasure."

"I still stand by that. Let me buy you a drink

and we can discuss the terms of our nonbusiness relationship." Jordan waved at Leo, the bartender, who probably had told him when Camilla would be off work.

"What?" She swallowed her panic as she looked around at the coworkers who would be staying another hour until closing. "Here?"

He lowered his head as though he was about to share a secret, and her pulse skipped a beat. "You would prefer somewhere more private?"

"No," she said, trying to ignore the way her knees buckled any time those dimpled cheeks were close enough to touch. "We can go somewhere very public and very well lit. Like the Splitting Lanes Bowling Alley, for example."

He threw back his head and laughed, causing the other servers and one of the sous chefs to look their way. Camilla wanted to sink into the floor. It was one thing to play make believe last night at a fundraising gala, but it was quite another to have her coworkers think she was seriously considering being used by the rich playboy with a reputation for breaking hearts. Or worse. That he was going to get into the restaurant business with her only in the hopes of also getting into her pants.

She grabbed his elbow and tugged him toward the door. "Come on. The Bronco Brick Oven is open for another hour and I'm starved."

The pizza place was a few buildings over in the recently gentrified district of Bronco Heights. What had once been feed mills and industrial factories and even a muffler repair shop were now upscale restaurants and boutiques made to look rustic and elegant at the same time with lots of restored wood, exposed brick, and metal-infused designs. She'd never understand rich people and their tastes.

He held open the door for her and she felt the warmth of his hand on her lower back. A shiver raced through her, making her think it was almost scary how her body reacted to his barest touch.

"This isn't a date," she reminded them both.

That didn't stop Jordan from asking the young waiter wiping down vinyl-covered menus if they could have one of the booths in the rear corner.

"So you've gotten me to sit down with you," she said when he took the bench seat across from hers. "Does that make me just another woman who can't resist the Jordan Taylor charm?"

"You shouldn't believe everything you read about me on social media." He flashed that playful grin again, and Camilla thought she should definitely believe every single word she'd read. "Can't a man meet a woman at a party and simply want to take her out and get to know her better?"

"When they meet under normal circumstances?

Yes. But the woman you met last night wasn't the real me."

"So then tell me about the real you." Jordan leaned his forearms on the table, as though he was actually interested.

"Well, for starters, I'm not the daughter of one of your dad's wealthy business associates. My parents aren't cattle barons or landowners who've been here for several generations. In fact, my parents immigrated here from Mexico thirty years ago. My dad doesn't get wine baskets after surgery, he gets a tater tot hot dish and a really bland tuna casserole that Mrs. Waters next door tried to make. I wear jeans and T-shirts when I'm not dressed for work." Camilla motioned to her standard white button-up shirt and black pants all the servers at DJ's Deluxe wore. Thankfully it was better than the misshapen brown polyester dress she'd worn when she'd worked at Waffle Station in college. "I don't wear ball gowns or high heels unless I borrow them. I'm a waitress and a student. I live in a tiny apartment above the post office in Bronco Valley. I drink beer on tap, not fifty-year-old single-malt Scotch."

The server returned at that exact minute, and Jordan asked, "Can we get a pitcher of Big Sky IPA?" Then he glanced at Camilla and added, "Beer on tap. Check. What else do I need to know?"

"That I never drink on an empty stomach," Camilla replied to him before turning to the server. "Can you also bring us the Italian chopped salad please? And an order of the garlic pesto twists?"

When the server left, Jordan leaned back in the booth, the sleeves of his dark blue shirt pushed up to his elbows. How did this guy look so casual no matter where he was or what he wore? In fact, even his appraising stare seemed casual, despite the fact that he was clearly sizing her up.

Finally, he nodded slowly. "So last night wasn't the real you?"

"Exactly."

"That would mean that the real you doesn't like dancing. Can't stand Beyoncé songs or the 'Cha Cha Slide.' The real you hates prime rib sliders—you ate six of them, by the way, so good job faking that—and you never lick your fingers when you spill au jus all over them. The real you doesn't smell like a wild field of lupines in the middle of June and doesn't have the widest and most compelling smile I've ever seen." Jordan's words had almost more of an effect on her than his silky eyes still drinking her in. "And the real you isn't at all passionate about the traditional Mexican restaurant you want to build using your grandmother's recipes and your hard-earned experience in the restaurant industry."

The pale ale arrived and Jordan poured her a

glass with the same ease he'd poured the Scotch last night. Clearly, everything came easily to him.

"Fair enough." She took the offered pint. "But Jordan, be honest. When was the last time you dated someone who didn't drive a luxury car?"

He pursed his lips and lifted his eyes to the ceiling as if he needed to think of a response.

She took back-to-back sips of the beer, slowly swallowing as she allowed him more time to come to the foregone conclusion. She exhaled and said, "Your silence speaks volumes."

"Maybe that's the problem," he replied. "I haven't been dating the right kind of women."

"According to those society columns you don't want me to believe, you've had quite a variety of ladies to choose from."

"Look, Camilla, my dating life is apparently an open book. You obviously know what you're getting into by going out with me. But I've never met anyone like you. I've certainly never dated anyone like you."

She lifted her eyebrows in doubt. "You mean someone in the working class?"

"I mean someone who seems to enjoy life as much as you do. Who has enough ambition to come to a party where she doesn't know anyone so that she can pitch her restaurant idea to strangers. Someone who kept me up all night thinking about her infectious laugh and when I could hear it again."

Her breath suspended in her rib cage. If she wanted to avoid going light-headed and weak in the knees, she either needed to get some food in her system or she needed to double down on her efforts to resist his charm. Although, it was becoming increasingly difficult to keep her guard up against this man when he said all the right things.

If only to keep herself on the defensive, she turned the conversation back to him. "How do I know you're not just some guy who enjoys slumming it with a girl from the other side of the tracks?"

Jordan's raised brow made her wonder if this guy ever took anything seriously. "First of all, Bronco Valley doesn't have any tracks. They all run north of the Heights." Then his mouth straightened and his jaw hardened. "And if anyone were to ever refer to me dating you as 'slumming it,' I'd personally kick their ass."

"Even your father?" she challenged. "I mean, obviously I don't condone violence toward anyone of an advanced age who clearly suffers from nearsightedness. But how would the wealthy Taylors feel about you dating an immigrant's daughter from Bronco Valley?"

Seeing the determination glinting in his

eyes, she suddenly wondered how she could've thought this multimillion-dollar businessman couldn't be serious when he needed to be. "I'd tell my family the same thing I tell them whenever they ask about my dating life. It's none of their business."

The chopped salad and the fragrant knots of perfectly baked dough topped with basil and parmesan arrived, and Jordan asked if she wanted to order anything else. She was starved after skipping lunch to run all those errands today, but she shook her head.

When the server left, Jordan asked, "How long did it take you to have me all figured out?"

She pointed her fork at him. "About five minutes."

"Because you knew my name and you knew my reputation based off some online articles." He slid a hot, cheesy twist into his mouth. Watching him, Camilla's stomach melted like the garlicky butter he'd just licked off his fingers.

"Also because I know guys like you. Rich boys who've never had to work hard for what they wanted." She shoved a forkful of salad in her mouth, not wanting to entice him the same way he was enticing her.

"You don't think I can work for what I want?"

"I'm sure you're a very good businessman, Jordan. I also read the financial articles about you, not just the society columns. Unfortunately, I'm not one of your business ventures or some associate who is open for negotiations."

"That's a good idea." He finished off the rest of his beer. "We should negotiate."

"I just said I wasn't open to that," she reminded him. But then her curiosity got the better of her. "What exactly do you want to negotiate?"

"Give me four weeks. Go out with me at least twice a week for four weeks and I'll prove to you that I'm not the guy you think I am."

"You're crazy." She chuckled, then realized he wasn't laughing with her. "You can't seriously think us dating is a good idea."

"Why not? Are you worried that you'll get too attached and fall in love with me?"

In love? Not a chance. But she was already recklessly attracted to him, so she did have some concerns about letting him get too close. Unfortunately, she'd inherited that Sanchez competitive gene and, like everyone else in her family, she'd never been able to back down from a challenge.

"I'll give you two weeks." She took another bite of salad, hoping she wasn't going to regret this. "Two weeks will be long enough for you to realize that we're way too different to be together."

And not so long that they risked getting their

hearts involved. Oh, who was she kidding? She was the only one at risk for that. But that didn't mean she wasn't determined to prove him wrong. Besides, if he could introduce her to some possible investors, then it would all be worth it.

"Three weeks," he countered before refilling their glasses and holding his up in a toast. "That's long enough for me to convince you that we have a chance."

"Fine. Three weeks." She clinked his glass with her own in agreement. "If you can even last that long."

Jordan checked his reflection in the rearview mirror a second time. He didn't want to look like he was trying too hard, but he also didn't want Camilla to think he didn't care. He'd been hoping for a weekend date, but Camilla insisted that Friday and Saturday were her busiest nights at work and she relied on the extra tip money.

He hadn't wanted to wait until the middle of the week to start their three-week agreement, so she suggested they jump in with both feet. Sunday night dinner with her family.

Really, it was more of a dare than a suggestion. One that Jordan had all too willingly accepted. After all, when was the last time he'd actually met the family of a woman he was dating?

Even when he already knew the parents—

like the Abernathys—he still avoided any setting that might suggest the relationship was at that sort of level. If he wanted to prove that Camilla was different from the women of his past, then he'd have to approach their relationship differently, as well.

The Sanchez family's house was in the heart of Bronco Valley. It was a modest one story in an older subdivision where many of the homes looked identical. Jordan had purposely driven one of the ranch trucks instead of his Tesla. Since his money was already an issue with Camilla, he didn't want to draw any more attention to it.

There were several vehicles crammed into the driveway and on the surrounding street, so he was forced to park three houses down. As he approached the front door, he could hear several male voices inside arguing about fouls and free throw lines. Jordan took a deep breath before lifting his hand to knock. Before he could, a slightly younger, shorter version of Camilla almost hit him with the door.

"Come on in. Camilla is in the kitchen with our mom and I'm on my way to the store to get more mangos." The woman passed by him as he stepped into the entry, then leaned around him to call out, "Even though everyone knows you can't get a decent mango in Montana this time of year."

"Stop yelling, Sofia." An older, redheaded version of Camilla came out of the kitchen, wiping her hands on an apron printed with the words Your Opinion Wasn't in the Recipe. "Mr. Granada always keeps a couple of ripe ones for me behind his checkstand."

"Hey, Dad," a guy Jordan's age wearing a blue Bronco Fire Department T-shirt said. He was sitting on the armrest of an oversized brown corduroy sectional and didn't take his eyes off the TV. "What else is Mr. Granada keeping behind his checkstand for Mom?"

"Knock it off, Felix. And sit on my sofa like a normal person," the obvious matriarch of the Sanchez family scolded before her eyes landed on Jordan. "Oh, hello. You must be Camilla's friend. I'm her mom."

"It's a pleasure to meet you, Mrs. Sanchez," he said, then passed her the bouquet of flowers he'd gotten from a flower shop on his way over.

Her smile was just as wide and enthusiastic as Camilla's as she beamed at the flowers. "Please call me Denise. Aaron, did you see Camilla's friend is here?"

A taller man with a neatly trimmed salt-and-pepper beard had already hefted himself up from a recliner chair and used a pair of crutches to limp toward them. Jordan hurried to meet the man halfway. "I'm glad to make your acquaintance, Mr. Sanchez."

Camilla's father took Jordan's hand in his bearlike grip and, unlike his friendly, petite wife, did not insist that Jordan call him by his first name. But he did say, "Welcome to our home."

"Thank you." Jordan shifted the cellophane-wrapped wine basket in his arm. "I heard you recently had surgery, sir, and thought I'd bring a little something to ease the recovery."

Mr. Sanchez's eyes brightened when he noticed the wine basket Jordan had asked Mac to order on Friday. "That Napa cabernet certainly looks way better than the vegan lasagna my physical therapist brought over last week."

"Where did everyone go…" Camilla's voice died out when she entered the room and her gaze landed on Jordan. How did she grow more beautiful every time he saw her? Her hair was twisted into a messy ponytail on top of her head, and she was barefoot in her fitted jeans and long-sleeved white tee. She pushed a loose curl behind her ear, leaving a streak of flour on her cheek. "You actually came."

Jordan's throat tightened as he tried to make his tongue work. "You invited me, remember?"

Felix stood up. "Don't mind Cam. She's never invited a boyfriend over before and is probably just as surprised as the rest of us that you actually showed up."

"I'm not surprised," Denise said, nudging her daughter. "*Mija*, why don't you introduce your friend to the rest of the family?"

"Right." Camilla cleared her throat. "Well, the guy who likes to embarrass me is my oldest brother, Felix."

Felix offered his hand then asked, "Can I get you something to drink?"

Jordan glanced down at the empty bottle in Felix's hand. "One of those would be great."

"One beer coming right up."

"Grab me a corkscrew while you're in there," Mr. Sanchez told Felix before taking the basket from Jordan's arm and limping toward his recliner. "Gotta let the wine breathe before dinner."

"The guy in the Utah Jazz jersey..." Camilla pointed to a lanky guy sitting on the edge of a faded floral ottoman. "The one who can barely look over here because he's too busy watching the game? That's Dylan."

Dylan offered a wave. "Sorry, man, there's only a coupla seconds left."

"And the one who is supposed to be correcting third-grade spelling tests is Dante."

"How can I grade anything when the Jazz are about to lose a home game and make Dylan cry like a little baby?" Dante said, but set aside the papers he'd been ignoring and stood up to shake Jordan's hand. "What was your name again?"

"Jordan Ta—" Before he could finish, a loud buzzer sounded from the TV and a chaos of yells erupted around him as everyone but Camilla rushed back to their spots around the weathered oak coffee table. Mr. Sanchez had the wine basket balanced on one knee and Mrs. Sanchez balanced on the other.

"What'd I miss?" Felix handed Jordan a beer as he rushed by. "Did they get the three pointer?"

"We're going into overtime, baby!" Dylan pumped a fist while Dante cradled his head in his hands and groaned, "No!"

Several voices spoke over each other at once, and Camilla gestured at the scene in the cozy living room. "So this is my family. I hope you like basketball."

"I haven't played in a while." Jordan took a sip of the cold beer, recognizing the label of a local brewery. "Football was more my thing in high school and college."

"Not so loud." She put a finger to her lips. "Last year, Sofia brought home a guy who said he only played tennis and you would've thought he'd said he only enjoyed kicking puppies."

"That boy was no good for Sofia," Mr. Sanchez, who apparently had tuned out Dylan and Dante's bickering, called out.

"You say that about every boy Sofia brings home," his wife tutted before kissing his forehead.

"Oh, come on, Mom," Dante added. "The guy's name was Winston and he drove a BMW convertible. In Montana. In winter."

"Dante's right." Dylan still hadn't taken his eyes off the TV screen as he finally agreed with his brother about something. "That's what happens when you guys let her get a job at that stuck-up clothing store in the Heights. She ends up surrounded by all those trust fund dudes whose daddies have to give them jobs because they have no real-world experience."

Wow. Jordan's collar suddenly felt a lot tighter as that last comment hit a little too close to home. Maybe it was a good thing he hadn't said his last name earlier.

"For the record," Camilla said as she turned toward her family and planted her hands on her hips, "nobody *let* Sofia get a job there. This isn't the middle ages. She is a grown woman who does what she wants and is perfectly capable of making her own decisions."

"Says the girl who is also working with those snobs in the Heights," Dante said before pointing at the television and yelling, "His foot never even touched the line!"

"He was totally out of bounds!" Dylan yelled back, resuming the brotherly squabble.

Camilla shot Jordan a look as though to say, *See. I warned you.*

But Jordan's own family—especially his uncles—were equally as passionate when it came to football. So sports rivalries were nothing new to him. Besides, the Sanchezes seemed welcoming enough. As long as they got to know him before finding out who his father was, everything should be fine. After all, he wasn't here to talk about himself. He was here to spend time with Camilla.

Or at least that was what he'd thought before she returned to the kitchen with her mom, abandoning him to watch the rest of the game with her father and brothers. He swallowed a few more sips of beer, settled into an open spot on the sofa and found himself cheering for a team of players he'd never shown much interest in before now.

Sofia came through the door with the promised mangos, which started another round of teasing about Mr. Granada at the store having a crush on their mother.

When the Jazz finally won, Mrs. Sanchez turned off the television before Dante and Dylan could argue about the postgame interviews.

"Better get the grill going, Aaron. This chicken isn't going to cook itself."

It was still clear and sunny for a fall day, so the family went outside to a faded wooden deck that held a long patio table and several mismatched chairs. The yard beyond the deck was only big enough for a fenced-off vegetable garden, a tidy patch of grass and a smooth concrete slab with a regulation-height basketball hoop at the end.

In the center of the table was a tray of freshly cut vegetables coated with lime juice and chili powder, a bowl of tortilla chips, and the best mango habanera salsa he'd ever tasted. All three Sanchez sons offered to grill the seasoned chicken so that their father could sit down, but the older man refused, insisting that he needed to get accustomed to the surgical boot.

Jordan, though, had a feeling that Mr. Sanchez's insistence on maintaining command over his propane grill had more to do with a father not quite ready to hand over control to his sons. Cornelius, who never even used the professional grade oven at home, suddenly became a master griller every time the Taylor uncles came over for a barbecue. His dad would've accused his kids of trying to put him out to pasture if anyone suggested he couldn't handle something he thought was his patriarchal duty.

That certainly was *one* thing Cornelius Taylor and Aaron Sanchez had in common.

Camilla eventually made her way outside and handed Jordan one of the two beers in her hand before taking the seat beside him.

"Are you overwhelmed yet?" she asked under her breath, and he had to catch his. If he'd thought she'd been stunning at the gala, seeing her relaxed grin and total ease in this environment had him thinking thoughts he shouldn't be thinking in the company of her parents and three big brothers.

"Quite the opposite," he replied. "Don't forget that I have a big family, too, especially when you count my Taylor cousins. But we can wait a few more dates before I subject you to all of that."

Camilla's smile faltered and her eyes went round before she blinked a few times. "Let's get through one awkward moment at a time before we get ahead of ourselves."

"Good call." He clinked his bottle of beer against hers and added, "For once, I'm going to sit back and enjoy tonight before strategizing for tomorrow."

Unfortunately, just when Jordan thought he was going to finally get some time with her, Dante produced a basketball and spun it on his finger. "Who's up for some two on two?"

"I'm down." Felix stretched his arms over his head. "I'll even take Jordan on my team."

"Are you sure you want to go against us, big brother?" Dante asked before sharing a look with Dylan. "You know what happened last time."

Jordan glanced at Camilla, whose lower lip twisted in doubt. She lowered her voice and said, "You don't have to play with them. Dylan and Dante would rather play against each other anyway."

"No way," Denise Sanchez said. "They fight too much when they play against each other. They either play on the same team or not at all."

Jordan felt everyone's stares as they waited anxiously to see how far he was willing to go to impress Camilla's family.

He stood up and she tugged on his hand. The excitement of her touch, though, was short-lived by her warning. "They won't go easy on you."

Was any phrase more crushing to a man's ego than that? Or more compelling?

Unbuttoning his flannel shirt, he smiled. "Good."

The match was close at first as Jordan paced himself and got a sense of his teammate and his opponents. Felix was good, but Dylan and Dante were way better than their older brother. They also got along surprisingly well when they had the same goal in mind.

Jordan left the very playful trash talking to

Felix, who gave as good as he got when it came to insults. Several times, Sofia and both parents seemed to be doubled over with laughter at the zingers and one-liners exchanged on the court. But amid the fun, there was also some serious competition. The game heated up as more baskets were made and more elbows were thrown. Mr. Sanchez called out the personal fouls—and there were several of them—from his spot behind the grill.

Halfway through the game, Jordan found his stride and learned how to read the younger brothers' passes and how to avoid Dylan's larger frame trying to box him out. They were playing to twenty-one and Jordan and Felix won the first game by only two points.

They won the rematch by ten.

Jordan was covered in sweat—and possibly a few tears from holding back his laughter—by the time they walked back to the patio table.

He snuck a peek at Camilla, hoping she didn't object to his soggy appearance. Not that he'd ever cared before about how he looked. Her eyes were locked on his damp white undershirt, though, and his chest muscles flexed instinctively.

Before things could heat up too much, Sofia threw them each a towel and Mrs. Sanchez passed out bottles of ice-cold water. She tsked sympathetically at her younger sons. "To help you wash down your loss."

"You could've at least cheered for us, Mom," Dante told her.

"That's what you get for underestimating our guest, *mijo*." Mrs. Sanchez laughed. "Besides, your father burned the last few pieces of chicken because he was too busy calling out advice for you and Dylan. You two needed all the help you could get against Jordan."

Camilla had neither cheered nor offered any words of advice, but Jordan had felt her eyes on him the entire time. Even now, as she openly studied him, a slow smile playing on the corner of her mouth. She pulled out the chair beside her. "I thought you were more into football."

"I am. But that doesn't mean I'm not good at other sports." He took a long pull from the icy cold bottle of water. The aching muscles in his back were already starting to disagree.

She drew up one knee as she turned in her seat toward him. "I have a feeling that you're good at everything you do, Jordan."

"You have no idea," he promised, meeting her gaze.

Chapter Four

What day works best for you this week?

Camilla read Jordan's text on Monday morning as she huddled under her down comforter in her studio apartment.

Yesterday afternoon, she'd thought that she'd finally get him to admit defeat when it came to pursuing this ridiculous three-week trial dating period. She'd thought he'd take one look at her family's humble home, meet her obnoxiously competitive brothers, have dinner on her mom's favorite—and unbreakable—melamine plates, and hit the pavement.

Instead, he'd beat her brothers at their favorite sport and talked about grilling temperatures with her father and washed those same unbreakable dishes with Felix, whose turn it was to clean the kitchen. He'd even agreed to stop by their mom's salon for a haircut that he didn't need but Denise insisted on.

How had he won over her family so quickly? Probably because they had no idea he was one of *those* Taylors from Bronco Heights. At one point, she'd whispered a warning to Jordan not to bring up his name in front of the rest of the Sanchezes—unless they wanted to get teased unmercifully like Sofia and her last boyfriend.

Not that Jordan was her boyfriend. Or anything close to it. In fact, they hadn't so much as held hands yesterday at her parents' house. Still, it was best to keep him from getting any grand ideas.

She typed back, Actually, this week isn't so great. I'm working as many shifts as I can and I'm behind on my reading for my Business Ethics class. Plus, I have to find time to drive to Missoula to meet with my academic advisor before Thanksgiving break.

She saw the three dots indicating he was typing. Thinking he would give up, she held her breath. Then let it out in an unladylike snort when she saw his response. What day? I'll see if I can use the company chopper and come with you.

So much for him not getting any grand ideas. She groaned before replying. It's only a two-hour drive. I don't need you to go to the trouble of booking a helicopter to impress me.

I was going there anyway to meet with one of our distribution representatives. It'll be easy to re-schedule my meeting for whatever day you need to go.

He used the word *easy* as though distributors would shift their entire schedules just to meet with him. As though helicopter pilots had no problem just idly sitting around waiting for Jordan to change flight plans on a whim.

But…

Camilla's old Toyota *had* seen better days, and she hadn't had time to drop it off to get serviced lately. Plus, she'd never ridden in a helicopter before…

No. She slammed her phone down on the soft mattress. She was being ridiculous to even consider the possibility. There was no way she was going up in the air with that man.

At least, that was what she told herself all day Monday. But after working a double shift on Tuesday and barely being able to keep her eyes focused on her textbook on Wednesday, Camilla decided not to look a gift horse in the mouth.

"Put these on so we can hear each other during the flight," Jordan said on Thursday morning as he passed her an oversized headset that covered her ears. The Taylor Beef helicopter was dark blue like their ranch trucks, with only a discreet TB logo on the tail of the aircraft. The inside was plush with wide leather seats and a minifridge between the rear seat and the control panel. "The pilot said we should be there in about thirty minutes. I arranged for a car service to pick you up at the airfield. I didn't know which building you had to go to on campus, so you'll have to give the driver directions. They'll wait for you there and then bring you to meet me for lunch after you're done."

"What if I'm done before you?" she spoke into the microphone of her headset just before the enormous propeller whirred to life.

"You won't be," he replied before giving the pilot a thumbs-up.

Her stomach dropped as they lifted into the air, and she grabbed at the most solid surface she could find: Jordan's thigh. Before she could remove it, his warm hand covered hers and held it in place. As their altitude increased, so did Camilla's wonder and excitement. She leaned toward the window, staring down at the rolling green hills below.

"It's beautiful from up here," she said, the amazement in her voice echoing back through the headset.

Instead of looking at the view below them, though, Jordan watched her instead. Her ears felt impossibly hot and she tried to keep from squirming under his appreciative stare. She licked her lips and pointed to a range of dense green trees. "Is that Flathead National Forest?"

Finally, he shifted his gaze to follow her finger. "Yep. You should see it after the first snow of the season. White as far as you can see. Maybe we can go up again in December."

Camilla shouldn't need to remind him that their three-week agreement would be over by then. Jordan was a smart man and probably knew full well that he was suggesting the impossible. She told herself to enjoy the experience and not think about the messy emotions that would likely come later.

So that was what she did. She sat back in the luxurious leather seat and marveled at the majestic view of the purple-tinged mountains and lush green treetops below her. Without releasing her right hand, Jordan passed her an orange juice from the small fridge. She was glad it wasn't anything stronger, because she didn't want to be tipsy or over-caffeinated when she met with her academic advisor, who also happened to be the assistant dean of the business school. When they started their descent ten minutes later, Camilla was almost disappointed the ride was over so soon.

She told herself the disappointment was due to the thrill of being so high up, and not because she would have to let go of Jordan's firm, warm hand.

Just as promised, there were two luxury SUVs waiting for them at the airfield. Camilla thanked the pilot, and Jordan told him that he'd text when they were ready to head back. Jordan held the door open for her and insisted on carrying her messenger bag with her laptop and notes. When one of the hired drivers opened the back seat door for her, Jordan quickly brushed his lips against hers and said, "See you at lunch."

Despite the chill in the air, she was still fanning herself as they drove toward the campus—in the opposite direction Jordan was heading. Camilla's advisor was running late, which gave her more time to calm her nerves and collect her thoughts. This meeting was only to review how she was doing on her Integrated Project. It wasn't as though Camilla was presenting her work or being graded on anything yet.

Just like with any other teacher, though, Camilla still wanted to be at her best. To have her

head in the game and absorb as much information as she could.

The problem was, all she could think about was
that parting kiss, which had been just as light as
the first, and whether there would be more where
that came from when she saw him again at lunch.

Jordan glanced at his cell phone for the eighth
time, trying to keep his eyes from glazing over as
his distributor in the Missoula office discussed
the innovations being made to the refrigeration
trucking industry. Normally, when it came to
Taylor Beef, Jordan insisted on knowing every
aspect of the daily operations that affected his
business. But he'd already read the reports be-
forehand and spoken with the truck manufactur-
ers. He'd also toured the Billings facility just last
week. Everything the distributor was saying was
already well-ingrained in Jordan's head. He'd already met with the department heads and rushed
through the presentations so that he'd be ready
to leave the second Camilla said she was done.

When the text finally came, Jordan thanked
the people sitting in the conference room for
their time and their commitment to Taylor Beef
and told the plant director not to bother walking him out.

His driver was already holding the back seat
door open when Jordan stepped outside. "Your

assistant sent me the address for your lunch res-
ervation, sir. The other driver has already picked
up Miss Sanchez and they're on their way."

When they arrived at the restaurant in down-
town Missoula, Jordan looked up at the red, white
and blue star-spangled sign plastered under the
roofline.

"Players?" Jordan mumbled to himself as his
head fell against the black leather headrest. This
better be a sports bar and not a strip club. Mac had
made that mistake once when Jordan had gone
on a business trip to New York and one of their
junior executive's social media posts had made
headlines back in Bronco. He breathed a sigh of
relief when he saw that this place had uniforms
that actually covered the employees' torsos. Still,
as he followed the hostess to something called
the MVP Lounge, he renewed his vow to never
let Mac make his restaurant reservations again.

"Sorry," he apologized to Camilla when he
found her seated at a high-top table. "I had actually wanted to take you to someplace a little
more…" He looked around at all the autographed
memorabilia and the twenty big-screen TVs
mounted on the walls broadcasting several different sporting events at once. "Intimate."

"I actually used to work at a sports bar just
like this when I was in college. The tips were
always great during playoff season."

"How long have you been a server?" he asked, pulling out one of the bar stools that were shaped like a catcher's mitt. Was he supposed to sit inside this thing and pretend he was a baseball?

Camilla giggled as he wiggled his butt uncomfortably in the weird-shaped seat. When she finally got control of her laughter, she answered, "On and off, about six years."

He did a few calculations in his head. "How old are you?"

"Twenty-seven. Isn't this all stuff we should've gone over on the first date?"

He dropped his chin and gave her his most charming smile. "I thought *this* was our first date."

"No, this is our fourth date," she corrected.

"You can't count some community fundraiser as a date."

"It's pretty telling how you refer to the fanciest gala I've ever attended as a community fundraiser—as though it was a school jog-a-thon or a church bake sale." She passed him a drink menu, which he set aside.

"Whatever you want to call it, that night doesn't count since we had barely even met."

"What about the following night when we had dinner at The Bronco Brick Oven?" she countered. "We even knew each other's real names by then."

"Still not a date." He held up his fingers to

count. "One, it wasn't planned. Two, I was still trying to convince you to go out with me."

Camilla rolled her eyes. "And I suppose dinner with my family didn't count as a date, either?"

"It was more of a date for me and Felix than it was for me and you. After all, I got to know him better than you that evening."

"Next you're going to tell me that our three-week agreement doesn't start until today, either." She leaned her forearms along the edge of the table as she studied him.

Jordan's mouth suddenly went dry, but he wasn't sure if it was from the way she was challenging him or from the way her V-neck sweater now framed the upper curve of her breasts.

"The agreement was six dates in three weeks. So if this is date number one, it also has to be week number one." Jordan tried to look as confident as he could in this ridiculous baseball glove-shaped chair as she playfully narrowed her eyes at him. "Don't blame me. I don't make the rules."

"Oh, it sounds like you make all the rules, Mr. Taylor. The rest of us have to play by them." Her words once again targeted his reputation, or his wealth, or any number of things that Jordan was slowly learning people didn't like about him. She softened the blow by adding, "At least you make the game interesting."

A server came to take their order. When Jordan asked if she wanted to split another pitcher of beer, Camilla replied, "I better not. I have to be at work by four."

After they ordered their iced tea, appetizers, and build-your-own burgers, he asked, "So, don't you want to know how old I am?"

"No, I already know how old you are. I wasn't the one who mistook you for someone else that first night."

"That's right. You know everything there is to know about me." When was he ever going to get her to see the real him, though? He hadn't even been able to be completely honest with her family about his last name, which was an unusual experience for Jordan, who normally was very proud of his family and his work at the company.

"Well, not everything," she admitted when their drinks arrived. "What exactly do you do for your dad?"

"Technically, I *do* work for my family's company, which is equally owned by my father and my uncles, by the way. But contrary to popular belief, I actually had to earn my position. My great-grandfather, the original Cornelius, started the precedent that any Taylor who wanted to be in the family business had to start at an entry-level position."

"So which entry-level position did you start at?" she asked.

"All of them." He saw her sympathetic expression and clarified, "And not because I kept messing up and having to switch departments, either. Obviously, I started in the product development department—which means I shoveled manure for the first year out at Taylor Ranch. Then my Uncle Victor promoted me to herding, which is not quite as glamorous as the old Westerns make it seem. Having a few of my cousins also working out in the pastures with me made for some fun and exciting stories, but I could only be a cowboy for so long before I had to move on to the next stage."

"You say *had to* move on." Camilla took a drink of her iced tea. "Is that another rule for the Taylor offspring?"

"Nope. We're allowed to work wherever we want as long as we start at the bottom. I liked herding, but I liked making business deals more."

"So that's when you started climbing the corporate ladder."

"Not exactly. The summer before I graduated college, I worked in the packing facility, which was my least favorite position for obvious reasons. As soon as I felt I had a good handle on how to raise and, unfortunately, get the cattle ready for distribution, I switched to the communications department. Once I got the hang of that, I moved on to accounting. Then to advertising, human resources, and I even worked with the legal team learning about contracts and negotiations."

"Wow." She blinked several times, her long lashes drawing his attention away from her full lips. "I really wasn't expecting all of that."

"Yeah, well, I guess that's because it's not the most interesting thing the social columns can write about me."

"Fair enough." She lowered her perfectly arched eyebrows. "So what exactly do you do now?"

"I'm vice president of operations. My Uncle Lester created the position for me since I'm one of the few people at Taylor Beef who has experience working in so many departments. My cousins call me the Smoother because whenever a manager or a client has a problem, I can usually get in there and smooth things out."

Camilla gave a chuckle. "Yeah, I'm sure that's not the only thing you're smooth at."

"What can I say?" Jordan shrugged. "It's a gift and a curse. But more of a gift when it comes to the business aspects of my life. So to answer your question, I still do a little of everything at the company, but now I have to go to a lot more meetings."

"Like today with the distributor?" she asked. "How did that go?"

As he answered, he was surprised he could remember everything he and Franco's team had discussed about the truck refrigeration and the updated shipping routes since he'd been distracted the entire time thinking about this upcoming lunch. When he finished, he asked, "Tell me about your meeting with your professor."

"It was the assistant dean, actually. She's my academic advisor for my Integrated Project. At first, I was just going to use the business model for my restaurant as my project, since I'd been working on the idea for years. But the more I got involved developing it, the more I realized that I could actually make this restaurant thing happen. So I was showing her what I'd developed so far."

He kept her talking about her restaurant and she lit up with enthusiasm as she told him about her vision for the location and the dining room layout and the types of food she wanted to serve. Camilla was so knowledgeable and so animated, quickly alternating between eating and talking with her hands, that he didn't see how any investor wouldn't want to throw all their cash at her.

They finished their lunch and Camilla excused herself to use the restroom. When she returned, she asked, "Are you ready to go? My shift starts in a couple of hours and I still need to stop by my apartment and change into my uniform."

"I just need to pay the check," he said, trying to get the attention of the server.

"I already took care of it," Camilla replied.

"When?"

"Before you got here." She pulled the strap of the messenger bag onto her shoulder, then pivoted and headed toward the door.

Catching up with her by the hostess stand, he cocked his head toward the server, who didn't run over to stop them from dining and ditching. "You paid the bill before you even knew what I'd want to order?"

"I guessed that you'd want a burger. The menu advertised the fact that they use Taylor Beef and you seem like a guy who takes quality control very seriously. It would obviously need to be loaded with bacon and cheese and all the toppings since I saw you fill your plate at my parents' house the other night and pile on as much stuff as you could onto such a small circle. Then I accounted for a side salad since you ate half of mine last week at the Brick Oven. I knew I'd want to try several appetizers, because the quality of the appetizers tells you a lot about a restaurant, so there was no guessing there. And you always drink whatever I'm drinking. So, even before you walked through that door, I knew it was going to be $42.83 before tax and tip."

"But why?" He followed her to the waiting car, mentally running through the calculations she'd just ticked off to realize she'd been exactly right.

"Because I work in the food industry and I've made a game out of guessing people's orders based on less information than I already had about you." She thanked the driver and slid across the back seat so Jordan could climb inside.

"No, I mean, why did you pay for the bill in advance?"

"Oh." Her lips spread into a self-satisfied smirk, lighting up her beautiful face in a way that made his rib cage tighten. "Because I also knew that you would try to pay for me, just like you paid for the car service and the helicopter, and dinner at the Brick Oven. Oh, and the wine basket for my dad, which was a nice touch, by the way."

"Well, I told you at the gala that I'd sent him one after his surgery." He shrugged, but the tightening in his chest didn't loosen.

"You mean back when you thought my father was Jose Balthazar?" Her smirk was now a full grin. He loved the way she wasn't afraid to tease him.

Contentment spread through him and he returned her smile. "I figured since you weren't going to let me forget about my mistake, I might as well follow through on that."

"Well, my dad loved it, so well played. Anyway, I didn't want you always paying for everything and I certainly didn't want to get into a standoff with you about it when the bill came. So I prepaid before you got the chance to outnegotiate me again. You're welcome."

She was right. He definitely would have insisted on paying for her lunch and she had been wise enough to cut him off before he even had the opportunity.

"I'm trying to remember the last time a woman bought me a meal," he finally said as he stared at her in amazement. "Thank you."

"It was my pleasure," she said, and his mind spent the rest of the ride thinking about all the other ways he'd like to bring her pleasure.

Once inside the helicopter for the return trip to Bronco, Camilla again reached for his hand during takeoff, but most of her attention was on the view from the window. Not only could he not remember the last time someone had paid for his restaurant bill, he also couldn't remember the last time he'd paid so much attention to the world below the propellers. Had Jordan really gotten so accustomed to luxury air travel that he'd forgotten to look away from his phone or his laptop during the flights? That he'd forgotten what it was like to sit back and simply enjoy the scenery?

Before they arrived back at the airfield, Jordan already knew that he wasn't going to be able to wait until after the weekend to see Camilla again. He said as much when he was walking her to her car.

"What are you doing tomorrow morning?" he asked, hoping he didn't sound as desperate as he felt.

"Laundry."

"Great." He opened her car door. "My last stepmother gave me this square tool that folds shirts perfectly. You should see my closet. It's an ode to organization and color-coded stacks. I'll bring it over and help you."

She sucked her lower lip between her teeth before answering. "Jordan, my studio apartment is probably the same size as your closet."

He knew she was baiting him again about the differences in their bank accounts, but he wasn't going to fall for it. "If this is your way of asking me back to your place so we can compare sizes, I'll gladly borrow a tape measure from one of the flight mechanics over there."

Lifting his eyebrows, he leaned in closer, and she playfully pushed him back. But instead of letting go, she kept her hands on his shoulders. "Don't you think it's a little too soon for you to come back to my place?"

"Nope," he said honestly, his deltoid muscles flexing impulsively under her touch. "But I would never push for an invite. You can have me over whenever you're ready."

"You know," she said, her thumbs driving him crazy with featherlight circles against his shirt, "when we negotiated our three-week deal, we never agreed to any of those terms you add in fine print at the end of the contract."

"So this thing between us is a business contract now?" Jordan tilted his head closer, careful not to lean forward too much and dislodge her mesmerizing hands.

Camilla shrugged one shoulder. "Well, I have a head for business and you have a head for business. So maybe it would keep things from getting too complicated if we set out our expectations ahead of time."

He glanced at her palms, which had strayed from his shoulders to his chest and were rising and falling with each steadying breath he took. "In that case, if you're going to distract me while we negotiate, I think it's only fair that I get the same advantage."

Matching her light pressure, Jordan placed his own hands on either side of her waist. He heard her quick intake of air, but she took a step toward him and asked, "So, we agree that this is date one out of six?"

"I'll concede that. For now." He already knew

that he'd want way more than six dates, but he still had time to convince her. "As long as you concede that the contract can always be extended upon mutual agreement."

She shook her head lightly, her hair rippling down her back as she smiled indulgently. "We'll see. Now what exactly constitutes a date? How do we define it?"

He looked up to the sky briefly before settling his gaze on her. "It should probably involve us spending time together. Alone."

"We haven't been alone today at all. We've either been in public or with drivers and pilots."

"I mean where we can have semiprivate, one-on-one conversations. And we should probably add that it needs to involve a full meal, since we both enjoy eating."

"If we're seen together in public too much, people are going to start talking."

He slid his hands behind her back, pulling her closer. "So let them talk."

Camilla let out a deep breath, as though he should already know full well all the reasons why she might not want to be seen with him. "So dates need to consist of semiprivate conversations and a meal. Anything else?"

"We should probably include some sort of physical contact, just so we can differentiate it as a date as opposed to a business meeting."

"Define physical contact." She was softly stroking the skin between his hairline and his collar, and he didn't think he could define anything if she kept touching him like that.

"Well…" He drew her even closer as he studied her turned-up face. "We should probably hold hands, maybe put our arms around each other on occasion."

"Like this?" she asked, her chest rising as it brushed against his own.

His pulse picked up speed. "Oh, we should definitely touch each other like this. And…"

"And?" Her heavy gaze slid to his lips.

"And we should obviously finish off with a goodbye kiss," he suggested.

Camilla didn't give Jordan the chance to simply get by with one of those soft, restraining kisses he'd teased her with in the past, though.

No, she rose up on her toes and pressed her mouth eagerly against his. The pressure of her firm lips opening beneath his filled him with a heady thrill that he didn't think could be matched. That was, not until she used her tongue to tentatively stroke against his as he welcomed her inside.

She settled her arms on his shoulders and cupped her hands behind his neck. His hands at her waist kept her close to him, but as he deepened the kiss, she arched against him.

Hearing her soft moan made his blood riot through his veins, but it also reminded him that they were in danger of going much further if one of them didn't stop soon. When he pulled away, he was slightly dazed and could feel his heartbeat thumping as though he'd just outridden a bull at his first rodeo.

"Like that?" she asked, her breathing coming in little pants.

"Exactly like that," he confirmed. "Although, I have a feeling that we just set the bar extremely high for our future goodbye kisses. I'll have my work cut out for me to match that level of wow on every single date. But I'm willing to keep trying until I get it right."

Her rib cage expanded above his grip as she shuddered. Then she straightened in his arms. "Like I said before, you're pretty good at everything you do. I don't think it's going to take much more practice."

His stomach tightened in anticipation at the thought of those practice sessions. There was no way he'd be happy with only six of these kisses.

He would definitely need to up their negotiations on the next date.

Chapter Five

"I don't think this counts as one of our dates," Jordan told Camilla on Saturday morning as they stood at the industrial-sized sink in the kitchen of the Bronco Valley Fire Station, washing multiple mixing bowls filled with pancake batter and a stack of syrup-covered dishes.

"Why not?" She laughed when he held a spatula the wrong way under the faucet and sent a spray of water right below his nose. "We're currently having a semiprivate conversation and there was a meal."

She hadn't taken him up on his offer to fold laundry together yesterday because no good would've come from it. At least she could tell herself that today they were actually giving back to the community.

"Serving the pancake breakfast at your brother's First Responders fundraiser doesn't count as a meal if we don't get to eat it ourselves," Jordan replied.

Ever since their goodbye kiss two days ago at the airfield, Camilla hadn't been able to stop thinking about the way his mouth had turned her completely inside out. Even now she could barely take her eyes off his lips. She used a dish towel to mop up the water sticking to the dark stubble along his jawline. "Volunteers eat *after* their shift."

"Good, because I'm starved."

Camilla tried not to drool over his biceps in that snug-fitting T-shirt, but he was up to his elbows in sudsy water and she was having a difficult time looking anywhere else. Besides his lips, which were also off-limits right now. In fact, she knew there was no way she could trust herself to actually be alone with him. That was why she'd suggested their next date be somewhere as public as possible.

Everyone from the Valley still came to the annual First Responders pancake breakfast, even when the station had moved to the new location near City Hall in Bronco Heights. Especially when they heard Jordan Taylor would be the one serving them. Actually, she didn't know for certain that word got out about Jordan being here, but when a group of young female teachers from Dante's school asked him to pose for a selfie with them, Camilla suddenly became aware of the fact that this was one of the largest turnouts she could remember in years.

She hadn't exactly accounted for any of those factors when she'd first promised Jordan that they could just eat pancakes with everyone else. Yet by the time Camilla and Jordan dried the last bowl, Felix had already turned off the griddle and there wasn't a pancake left in sight.

Jordan surveyed the spotless kitchen. "Looks like you still owe me a meal."

Working a volunteer shift with Jordan could be passed off as a charitable coincidence if people happened to spot them talking to each other. But if everyone saw them sharing breakfast at the diner next door, people in town would definitely start talking. It was already bad enough some of her friends had texted her with screenshots of the Denim and Diamonds gala Facebook page, which had posted pictures of Camilla and Jordan dancing together. The more people who suspected they were actually dating meant more people would know when Jordan eventually dumped her.

"We could grab a doughnut and a coffee at the bakery next door," she suggested.

Jordan pursed his lips playfully before slowly shaking his head. "Nope. The terms of our agreement were for a full meal. Only a five-year-old would consider an apple fritter to be a full meal."

"Fine." Camilla sighed. "My apartment is only a few minutes away. I'll cook you breakfast, but the goodbye kiss takes place outside."

"You don't trust yourself to kiss me again in private?" He slid his lower lip between his straight white teeth, and the wobbly feeling in Camilla's legs made her realize that she was perfectly justified in not trusting herself around the man in public, either. But she wouldn't admit as much.

"I'm just outlining the fine print, remember?"

"Got it. Does it say anything in there about me getting to keep this apron?" he asked.

She looked at the damp T-shirt sticking to his torso underneath. Maybe it was a better idea for him to keep as many layers on as possible. "No, but I think the fire station will give you a sweatshirt in exchange for a small donation."

She'd make the donation herself if it would stop her from staring at his broad shoulders in that thin cotton fabric.

Leaving the fire station, they only had to

drive a short distance to her apartment, a studio on the second floor of the Bronco Post Office. Many of the government agencies had been relocated to the Heights recently, but since the post office was a federal building, Aaron Sanchez had led the charge on keeping his workplace on this side of town.

As they exited their respective cars parked below her apartment, she realized that Jordan almost looked…normal. He wasn't wearing his designer tux or his tailored work shirts or his expensive hand-tooled cowboy boots. Instead, his faded jeans, sneakers and recently purchased blue hooded sweatshirt with the BFD logo proudly displayed on his chest made Jordan Taylor appear as though he actually belonged here in Bronco Valley.

It probably would have been safer for her to see him totally shirtless.

Camilla had no business thinking that someone like him would ever simply fit into her life. Something would eventually go wrong and he'd move back to his own world. The threat of impending disaster settled on her shoulders as she led him up the steps to her apartment.

Nevertheless, she persisted.

Her fingers trembled as she unlocked the door. The excitement of being this close to him made her lightheaded, thereby counteracting the emotional weight of her decision to invite him inside.

Contrary to what she'd boldly assumed at the airfield the other day, Camilla's studio apartment *was* in fact bigger than Jordan's walk-in closet back at the ranch house. But not by much, he calculated.

Jordan sat on one of the chairs at the tiny table in the corner between her kitchen and a blue upholstered love seat crammed with too many throw pillows to accommodate one full-sized human, let alone two.

"How do you pronounce it again?" he asked before shoveling another bite of well-done eggs into his mouth.

"*Chilequiles*. There's lots of variations, but this one is fried corn tortillas smothered in cheese and my dad's homemade salsa. This is one of my grandma's recipes that I'm toying with for my restaurant. It's much better when the egg on top is sunny side up, but broken yolks are my cross to bear."

"It's perfect," he insisted before taking another huge bite and letting the flavors of tomato and spices and tortilla come together in his mouth.

"Don't look so impressed." Camilla sat across from him, but the table was so narrow, their knees kept bumping underneath. "I rarely have time to grocery shop, and this particular recipe requires the fewest amount of ingredients and the least amount of skill. I don't really cook, even when it's my turn on Sunday evenings with my parents. I'm usually in charge of kitchen prep and I've picked up a few tricks when it comes to plating the food. But this is about as far as my expertise goes."

"You might not want to mention that to the future investors of your restaurant. Aren't world famous chefs the trend right now?" he asked.

"I don't want trendy. I want good service and great food. A place where people can go on a first date or on a seventeenth date. Special, but also ordinary, if that makes any sense."

Jordon shook his head. "There is nothing ordinary about you."

"That all depends on how you define it. If I were to come visit you at *your* house, I suppose that I would stick out like a sore thumb." She speared a mound of tortillas and egg on her fork. "But here in Bronco Valley, I assure you that I am very ordinary."

Like the Sanchez home, Camilla's apartment was stuffed with books—both business-related and an array of fiction paperbacks—and framed family photos that were not staged by professional photographers. Not everything matched, but it was clean and interesting and full of her personality. The main house on the Taylor Ranch was also full of history and personality, but not quite the same amount of warmth. At least not anymore. When Jordan, Brandon and Daphne were little, Cornelius had been a busy, yet doting single father who'd hung up his children's artwork on the fridge and didn't mind bicycles and footballs left on the front lawn. But then his kids got older and his wives got younger and a team of interior decorators convinced the patriarch of the family that his home should reflect his standing in the community.

Yet that didn't mean Camilla couldn't be equally as comfortable at the ranch. After all, the Taylor home was at its best when it was filled with people, like it had been the night he'd met her.

"I highly doubt you would stick out at my house." Jordan said. "In fact, you've already been there and as I recall, you fit in quite well."

She crossed her arms over her chest. "That was before you knew who I was."

"But *you* knew who you were and you seemed to be having a good time," he said.

"Going to a massive party in a tent on your property is a lot different than going inside your actual home."

"Prove it," he suggested.

"Prove it to who? I already know what will happen."

"Prove it to me. When's your next day off?"

"Tomorrow." Camilla narrowed her gaze. "Why?"

"Because I want you to come out to the ranch and let me show you around. It's actually the best time to visit because most of the employees have the day off, so it's usually just the family there. It's the perfect time to show up and just be yourself."

"Fine. But make sure the private chef leaves us something to eat so it can count as one of our dates."

"You don't think I can cook something for you?" he challenged her.

"Can you?" She lifted one brow.

"I can if it involves meat and bread and sandwich toppings."

"With that kind of promise, how do I say no?"

For the second time that day, he helped her wash the dishes, even though this kitchen was barely big enough for them to stand side by side, which he actually preferred.

Her apartment was so comfortable and so inviting, he wanted to kick back on her love seat and settle in for an afternoon nap while she studied, then later watch her get ready for her shift tonight at DJ's. But Jordan knew better than to wear out his welcome. He wanted to leave her wanting more.

"I guess I better take off so you can get to work," he said, balling up the wet dishcloth in his hand.

"I'll walk you to the door," she offered.

"Only to the door?" He lifted the corner of his mouth. So maybe he didn't want to leave her wanting *that* much more. "What about that goodbye kiss being in public?"

"It's probably not a good idea to do it where everyone can see us." Her brow was furrowed as though she was seriously contemplating it. "How about right outside my door? It overlooks the side alley and there shouldn't be too many people passing through there."

He followed her outside to the small balcony landing, where the stairs led to a parking area below with her Toyota and two postal trucks. The second she turned around, he didn't wait for her to make the first move.

This time he kissed *her*, pulling her in close as he cupped his hand around her neck, cradling her head. He'd let her lead on that kiss yesterday, using every ounce of his control to hold himself still as she explored his mouth. Now he was returning the favor.

His tongue stroked and caressed and promised that he was more than capable of filling her every need. In response, she pressed her body to his, straining against him as she let out a soft gasp followed by an even deeper moan. Hearing her sounds of desire only heightened Jordan's already growing arousal. It was obvious that if they continued, he'd soon have her against the open door frame. Blood was pounding in both his ears and his lower extremities when he finally pulled his mouth away and rested his forehead against hers.

It took several seconds of controlled breathing for him to trust himself to open his eyes and look at her. Satisfaction filled his chest as he noted her dilated pupils. It took more patience than he thought he possessed to not pull her in for another kiss. Instead, he asked, "So, we'll continue this tomorrow?"

"Maybe not *all* of this," she replied, then tentatively touched her full lips. "I've got to practice some restraint."

He put his finger under her chin, forcing her to meet his eyes. "Don't restrain yourself on my account. I like you just the way you are."

"That's what I'm afraid of," she murmured, then stepped backward and closed her front door.

Jordan's eyes took inventory of the house that resembled a five-star dude ranch rather than an actual residence where real people lived. Hell, compared to Camilla's apartment, this place felt like a damn museum.

He'd grown up here and it had always felt just like…well…home. It was all he knew. Wait. That wasn't exactly correct. The "kids wing," which contained the original bedrooms, felt like home because they were the least changed rooms in the house. It was also the area, other than the office building, where Jordan spent the most time.

When Cornelius divorced his first wife, he'd hired an architect and a general contractor to expand the floorplan. He'd said that it was high time to update their home, but Daphne had told her brothers that it felt like their dad was trying to erase his past with their mother. When he met his second wife, he'd brought in an interior decorator to showcase some cooked-up vision of a "modern Western vibe"—whatever that meant. After a second divorce, Cornelius hired a different interior decorator to redo the house, and soon a habit was formed. Every time Jordan's father suffered some sort of break-up or emotional setback, the old man added onto the house—making it grander than before—as a way of reaffirming his family's heritage and, in his mind, his value.

If Jordan wanted to convince Camilla that he was no different from her, then the formal entry was not the place to welcome her to his family home. He could invite her straight into his bedroom, the least ostentatious of all the rooms, but that might give her the impression that he was trying to seduce her. That left only one other choice.

Crossing the stately front porch, he headed across the circular gravel driveway and kept himself busy inside the stables as he waited for her arrival.

After their intense kiss yesterday, he'd gone straight to his office and buried himself in the latest reports on increasing the sustainable energy resources at all the Taylor Beef packing facilities. He'd been in need of an outlet to redirect his own energy, and going to work kept him from thinking about Camilla's lips and how they'd matched his so perfectly. The distraction had worked for the first hour. The rest of the night had been a struggle to focus on anything but her.

He was closing the paddock gate when he heard her engine shut off, and a thrill shot through him. She exited her car wearing faded jeans that perfectly hugged her curves in all the right spots, an old pair of tan cowboy boots, and a hooded sweatshirt that said University of Montana.

"You were right," she said as he walked around the fencing toward her. "This place certainly looks different without the huge party tent and all the cars. Where is everyone?"

"My dad and Jessica are at church, which is usually followed by brunch at the Association. I have no idea where my brother, Brandon, is."

"Only four of you live here?" At first she sounded amazed. Yet, there was no missing the teasing in her tone when she nodded at the house on the other side of the driveway and said, "Are you sure there's enough room for everyone?"

"Well, we also have employees who live on-site." He didn't admit that the stable hands stayed in the bunkhouse and the household staff had private quarters not attached to the main house. "But most of them have today off."

"Where are your uncles and their families? I thought all the Taylors lived on the compound."

"My dad, being the oldest, inherited the main house, and then each brother got their own corner of the ranch for their family spreads. We could spend the entire day exploring the property and still not run into any of them."

Camilla let out a small whistle. "Quite the kingdom. Is this the part where you impress me by showing me around?"

"No. I already know you won't be impressed by any of that. This is the part where I see if you can saddle your own horse. Did you borrow those boots?"

"Unlike the last time I came here, these particular shoes are actually my own." She stomped some dirt off one of the heels. "My dad grew up around horses in a small town outside of Guadalajara. He insisted that if his children were going to grow up in Montana, then they needed to know how to ride. We spent summers on my uncle's ranch in Jalisco and, during the rest of the year, all of us kids took lessons when my parents could afford it. In fact, not to toot my own horn, but I even did some barrel racing in high school and was the junior rodeo queen at the Bronco State Fair back in the day."

"Really?" He shook his head as she surprised him once again. "My family sponsors the Future Farmers of America building at that fair every year."

"I know." Her pointed look conveyed the unspoken words. Everyone knew who he was, yet he didn't have a clue who most of them were. Had he really been that out of touch with his own community?

"I've never been riding with a high school rodeo star before," he said, not regretting his decision to meet her away from the unrelatable wealth and privilege of the main house. "I better get you on a horse to prove you've still got it."

The challenge was exactly what Camilla needed to turn her attention away from the non-stop thoughts of continuing yesterday's kiss. Or of how amazing Jordan looked in that gray cowboy hat. It was no surprise that he obviously belonged on this ranch just as much as he belonged in the board room. It was getting harder and harder to prove that their worlds were too different when the man was like a damn chameleon fitting in everywhere he went.

She followed him into the stables and stood on the lower rungs of a stall as he saddled the horses he'd already chosen for them to ride. "Do they have names?"

He stroked the white mare's nose just above her bridle. "This little beauty is Leia, named after the princess, obviously."

"And I'm guessing the black stallion is named Darth?" she asked. "After the guy with the mask and the red light saber?"

"Actually, it's Palpatine, after the emperor of the dark side." Jordan handed her a set of reins. "I bet your social media sources didn't tell you I was such a big *Star Wars* fan, did they?"

"Wait." She took a cautious breath while trying not to compare the size differences between the two animals as she walked between them. "I'm riding the big black stallion and *you're* taking the smaller female horse?"

"Don't let his name fool you. Palp is a real sweetheart and will go anywhere you ask. Leia, on the other hand—" the white mare snorted at

Jordan and then pranced to the side as he tried to lead her out of the stable "—is exactly like her namesake. A real rebel, aren't you, girl?"

Camilla used the stirrup to mount the stallion easily enough despite how high off the ground she was. It took Jordan two tries and some sweet talking before Leia finally let him on her back. There was a whole stable full of animals he could ride, yet he insisted on taking the one who would give him the most trouble. Because of course he would.

As they rode their horses to the dirt trail heading east, Camilla took another glance over her shoulder at the house that didn't look any smaller from this distance. "Your parents must love the fact that you still live at home."

Jordan adjusted his hat. "It's just what we Taylors do. It's practically ingrained in us from birth. We work in the family business and live in the family home until we get married. I mean, not Daphne, of course, because she's smarter than all of us. But every other Taylor for the past several generations has done it."

"My parents are the same way. Minus the global family business part, obviously. But if they could've kept all of us at home, they would have. As you saw, though, our house is a bit more cramped than this one. By the time I finished college, I was too accustomed to living on my own and, even though it would've saved me a ton in rent money, I resisted their attempts to entice me back home. Although, it's such a small town I end up running into someone from my family pretty much every day. So it still kinda feels as though we all live together."

She watched his face beneath the brim of his hat, but he kept staring off straight ahead. "When my dad and Jessica first got married a couple of years ago, it seemed like the perfect time to move out. To give the newlyweds their space and all that. But then Daphne beat me to the punch and I didn't want Jessica to feel like we were all leaving because of her."

"So she's not the evil stepmother?" Camilla asked. Thankfully, Palpatine was docile enough that she could hold the reins loosely.

Jordan, on the other hand, kept a tighter hold on Leia, who kept sidestepping toward them, all but challenging the stallion to go faster. "Nah, she's nice enough and means well. But she tries too hard to please my dad instead of putting him in his place. It's like those signs at the campgrounds near Yellowstone Park warning people not to feed the bears because it only makes the bears more bold and more dependent on having their needs met. Jessica is the inexperienced camper who feeds the bear."

"Interesting analogy." Camilla appreciated the

fact that Jordan wasn't badmouthing the woman, even though many in his position could resent the fact that their father was married to someone so much younger. "But even more interesting is the fact that you've been to a campground."

"I'm not so pampered that I haven't been camping," he told her.

She gestured at the full trees and rolling green hills surrounding them. "No, I mean, why would you go to a campground when you have the great outdoors in your own backyard?"

Leia seemed to want to pick up speed and Camilla didn't believe in taming anyone or anything's spirit. So she nudged Palpatine faster and they cantered beside each other until they reached the crest of a hill that overlooked the house and several miles of pastures, which probably only represented half the Taylor holdings.

She was so blown away by the view that Camilla sighed. "Your ranch is truly beautiful."

He nodded, for once agreeing with her. "Obviously, I can't take credit for something I was born into. But I do love living here. Whenever my old man was going through a divorce or had a business deal fall through, being able to saddle a horse and get away on a ride was one of the few things that made living in his shadow bearable."

"If it's so frustrating living with your dad and working with him, why don't you take a page out of Daphne's book and move out? Surely Jessica would understand by now that it's not her."

"I've thought about it. Many times. In fact, lately I've been toying with the idea of getting a place in BH247—you know, that new condo complex in Bronco Heights—for no other reason than to stand in solidarity with Daph so she's not the only Taylor living off the ranch. I could even start a ranch of my own, but that would really send my father over the edge. And as overbearing as he can be, I do love him and don't want to be the one responsible for giving him high blood pressure. Besides, when I'm not at the office, I have the eastern suite of rooms to myself and a full-time cook and housekeeper to take care of everything else. If you ever meet my assistant, Mac, you will believe me when I say I hate hiring new staff."

"Gee. Only the eastern suite to yourself? How do you even manage?" she asked sarcastically with a friendly undertone. Instead of being properly chastised, though, he flashed those dimples and wiggled his dark eyebrows.

"See? You're the only person I've dated who will tell me things straight, no sugarcoating. I need that kind of honesty in my life, Camilla." Leia snorted, then whinnied, as though in agreement. "This is why you're good for me."

"Maybe so." She turned Palpatine around,

ready to let the antsy white mare beside them finally have the run she'd been itching for. As she took off racing, Camilla added to herself, "That doesn't mean you're any good for me."

Chapter Six

As they returned from the ride, Camilla saw the luxury car parked next to her older model compact sedan. Her heart rate had already been elevated from the fast pace Jordan and his mare had set. But when she saw who was sitting inside the vehicle, her pulse skipped a few beats. And not in a good way.

She caught the slight crease on Jordan's forehead before he managed to quickly wipe it away. He let out a breath, and kept his horse moving forward. "Looks like they skipped brunch, after all."

Cornelius Taylor and his much younger wife

were exiting the vehicle as they rode up, and Camilla's stomach twisted into a thousand knots. She expected Jordan to avoid the couple by cutting behind the corral and riding toward the rear of the stables. But he continued toward the driveway, giving her no choice but to follow.

Jordan dismounted first, which allowed Camilla to hear Jessica whisper to a squinting Cornelius, "I think it's one of Jordan's lady friends."

The older man apparently needed glasses more than he wanted to admit because with his wife's explanation, his face went from slightly annoyed to almost welcoming, and Camilla immediately wondered if he was about to put on an act for a visiting guest.

"Dad. Jessica." Jordan greeted each of them as Camilla dismounted by awkwardly sliding down Palpatine's very tall frame. "I don't know if you remember Camilla from the Denim and Diamonds fundraiser the other night?"

"Of course." Cornelius smiled at her, his perfectly set teeth very square and very white. "You're Jose's daughter."

"No, Dad. This is Camilla Sanchez, not Balthazar."

"I'm Aaron and Denise's daughter," Camilla felt obliged to point out to this man, who seemed to take so much stock in family legacies.

"Of course," Cornelius said with a confident

nod, although Camilla was certain he didn't have a clue who her parents were.

Nobody said anything for a few awkward moments and then Jessica, probably in an attempt to break the tension, said to Camilla, "I really loved the dress you wore to the gala. The gold one? Several people commented on a picture of it on my social media post asking who the designer was."

"Oh. Thank you. I…um…don't really remember." Which was truthful enough without admitting that she'd actually borrowed the dress.

The silence stretched between them again and Camilla pressed her lips together as she prayed that Jordan wasn't suddenly regretting inviting her to the ranch. Seeing Jordan around his family would be much more eye-opening than seeing him around hers. She hoped he wouldn't start acting like a kid who'd been caught with his hand in the cookie jar. The good news was, his face certainly didn't show a trace of shame. But then again, it never did.

"So, you're back from church early," Jordan finally said.

"Your father thought today's sermon on forgiveness was—" Jessica started, but Cornelius used his elbow to lightly nudge her arm.

"The sermon was so boring I could barely stay awake. It didn't help that Jessica kept me up half the night watching those home decorating reality shows she loves. You know how women are, son. You can give them all this—" he spread out his arms to encompass the massive house "—but still they want more."

Thankfully, Jordan didn't admit that he in fact knew how women were. Nor did he display an ounce of guilt for bringing a commoner like her to the Taylors' royal palace. His smile was polite, despite the fact that it lacked all his usual charm. "I was just about to invite Camilla inside and make her a sandwich. Would you like to join us?"

Camilla glanced down in time to see Cornelius briefly squeeze his wife's hand. She gave her husband a reassuring pat on the arm. "Actually, we should both probably have a little rest."

"Nice meeting you, Carol," Cornelius said before turning toward the front door.

"Dad, it's *Camilla*," Jordan corrected him. "Jeez."

He took off his hat to run his hand through his hair and probably didn't see Jessica mouth the word *sorry* to Camilla before following her husband.

"Well, that was awkward," Jordan offered, staring at the older man walking away. "My dad is usually way more charming. He must have really hated that sermon on forgiveness, especially since the minister's wife volunteers regularly at Daphne's animal sanctuary."

Camilla didn't want to point out that Cornelius Taylor's rift with his daughter hadn't kept him from smiling at his unexpected guest until *after* he'd found out that Camilla wasn't in fact related to the Balthazars. That was when the older man stopped any pretense of being charming. However, pointing out such a thing would only compel Jordan to attempt to prove her wrong, which would in turn bring more attention to an already awkward situation. So she just kept quiet as she walked her horse toward the stables to cool him down and give him some water.

Jordan, with Leia in tow, caught up to them. "I can understand why you wouldn't want to come inside for a sandwich now. Why don't I drive you into town and we can grab something to eat?"

Camilla stretched her back. It'd been a while since she'd ridden a horse, and she still needed to do some errands and even a bit of homework before dinner at her parents' house tonight.

"Maybe we should just call it a day."

"Sure, if you want." Jordan's agreement came a bit too readily as he tethered his mare to a post near a water trough. "But if we don't eat, then it doesn't count as a date."

So *that* was his game. She gave a snort of disbelief before picking up a currying brush. "Remind me how we came to the conclusion that our dates have to include food?"

"Because you like food?" He smiled at her.

"Do you want to rephrase that?"

"Why?" He dumped some oats into a hanging bucket for Leia, who immediately began chomping. "This old gal likes food, too. It's nothing to be ashamed of."

Camilla watched him caress the horse's silky nose as he murmured sweet words to her. A ping of envy darted through her as she thought about the way his very capable hands had similarly stroked her yesterday during their goodbye kiss.

She wasn't actually jealous of a horse, was she?

Leia, probably like many females before her, abandoned her treat to nuzzle against Jordan's hand. Well, Camilla certainly wouldn't be like the contrary mare and choose a little physical affection over a good lunch.

"That's because food is more reliable than men." She made eye contact with the horse, who continued to nuzzle against Jordan, refusing to be shamed. Camilla pointed a finger at the mare. "If you ever had the cornbread slathered in homemade honey butter they serve over at the BBQ Barn, you'd know that already."

Jordan laughed. "Looks like we're going to the BBQ Barn, then."

* * *

"So, what do you have planned after this?" Jordan asked when Camilla wiped her hands on a paper napkin from the dispenser. Instead of handing her another one, he used his thumb to wipe the tangy sauce off her cheek. He would've used his tongue if there wasn't anyone else in the restaurant.

"I'm supposed to go to my parents' house tonight. But after all those ribs, who has room for dinner?"

He looked at his watch, not quite ready to say goodbye. "I mean between now and then?"

"A nap sounds good." She pushed away from the wooden picnic-style table. "But I'm worried that if I fall asleep now, I'll end up in a food coma and won't wake up until tomorrow."

"So then it's up to me to keep you moving and alert. How about a basketball game?" he asked.

She held her still flat stomach and groaned. "Are you crazy? I *feel* like a basketball that just got slam-dunked."

"Not to play," he laughed. "To watch. My assistant is filling in as a substitute youth coach over at the rec center and she has a game today. It would mean a lot if we came out and supported her."

"You know, my dad is the ref for those basketball games. Or at least he was. He took off this season because of his bunion surgery. He's been telling our neighbors all about that wine basket, by the way. He didn't earn any points with Mrs. Waters when he told her it was way more therapeutic than her casseroles."

"I'll have to send him another one, then. Maybe one to Mrs. Waters, as well."

She rolled her eyes. He was getting used to the gesture whenever she wanted to convey that he was being over the top.

Before she could give him another excuse about being busy, he stood up and grabbed their plastic trays. "Come on. I'll drive."

She hadn't wanted to leave her car at the ranch, so he'd followed her into Bronco Valley and found a parking space a few rows away in the lot outside of the restaurant that was actually housed in an old barn. But now that they were so close to their next destination, there was no sense in taking both cars.

"Didn't there used to be a library here?" he asked as they drove by a single-story building that looked to be abandoned. "I remember having to do a report in middle school on the founders of Bronco, and my dad's secretary brought me over here to do research."

"I practically lived at that library when I was a kid." When Camilla smiled, it was contagious. "We would walk there after school and do our homework and read until my mom got off work. But then the city council voted to move all the government buildings—except the wastewater treatment plant, obviously—closer to Bronco Heights, where all the new developments were going in. They thought it made the town look more inviting. A group of us kids in the neighborhood protested, but you know the golden rule."

"What's the golden rule?" Jordan asked as he made a right turn.

"The guys with the gold make the rules." She slid her sunglasses onto her face, but not before he caught a glimpse of the defeat in her eyes. "After they moved all the books, a group of teens decided to throw a party in the abandoned building. The bonfire got out of control and did quite a bit of internal damage. It looks fine on the outside so nobody is complaining about it being an eyesore. The city council doesn't want to spend the money to make any repairs to the inside, not that anyone is offering to buy it since everyone seems to be building their businesses in the Heights now. So it's been sitting vacant for a while."

"How do I not know about this fire?" he asked, tapping his fingers on the steering wheel. "And before you say that I'm out of touch with our community, I'll have you know that I do pay attention to the news, and I think something like that would've at least made the papers."

"My brother Felix was one of the kids. He was still in high school at the time. He's thirty now, so that means you were probably away at college when it happened."

"Still. As a local businessman, I go to city council meetings a few times a year and never saw…" His surprise gave way to an underlying sense of shame as he realized what should've been obvious before now. "Hell. I can't believe I haven't noticed the town having a new library over in that complex."

They were at a four-way stop, and Camilla lifted up her sunglasses as she faced him. "Jordan, when was the last time you actually *went* to the library?"

The truck behind them honked, so Jordan was forced to return his eyes to the road. He had no idea if she was teasing him or not. "I actually went to library on my college campus once or twice to study."

"Yeah, well, the people in the Valley used this library more than once or twice. Some of them actually depended on it for after-school programs and the free tutoring and even internet access. Now if they want to go to the library, they have to find a way to get to the Heights.

The people with the most need for it now have less access to it."

Wow. His shoulders sagged and his throat felt thick and heavy. While he'd recently appreciated seeing the world through Camilla's eyes, up until now, he'd focused on the simple pleasures he took for granted. He hadn't wanted to give much thought to the necessities in life that he'd also taken for granted.

He pointed to one of the town's original buildings with weathered wood siding painted a shocking shade of bubble gum pink. "At least Cubby's is still here. We used to go there for malts and triple-decker sundaes after football games on Fridays nights."

"So did we!" Camilla smiled again, and Jordan's world suddenly righted itself. "It's still a madhouse on Friday nights. Especially when the high school has a home game. I think the Cubbison family got it approved as a historical monument, so the town has to keep it now."

They passed the market where the checker kept the extra mangos behind the register, then her mom's salon, which was one of the more modern-looking buildings in this neighborhood. He ran his hand through his hair. "Your mom didn't have time for me last week, so I had to schedule an appointment for Wednesday."

"I know. She told me all about it, probably

in the hopes I'll come help her at the shampoo bowl."

"You're a hairdresser, too?" Jordan asked, though at this point he wouldn't be shocked. He'd already found out that she was an MBA student, a restaurant entrepreneur, an amazing dancer and a rodeo queen.

"No. But when she was first starting out, she used to pay me and my brothers five bucks on Saturdays to ride our bikes over to the salon after we finished our chores so that we could help her sweep up hair and fold towels. She's built her business up a lot since then and has several stylists working for her now. But she still keeps our bikes in the garage and often reminds us that if we ever need to make a few extra dollars, we can pedal on over."

"It must've been nice to be able to ride everywhere." He pulled into the parking lot at the rec center. "Growing up, we always felt like we were stuck out on the ranch."

"Jordan, I was just on your ranch. I saw all the trails and the heated swimming pool. If the stable full of horses wasn't enough to get you from place to place, you also have ATVs." Camilla put her hand to her chest in a dramatic fashion. "Please tell me what a hardship it was to be stuck out there as a kid."

"I'm not saying it wasn't nice," Jordan corrected himself. After that conversation about the library, he knew he didn't have room for complaints. "I'm just saying we didn't have any neighbors nearby. We were kinda stuck out there unless we were at school. We couldn't just hop on a bike and go to our friends' houses. Or walk down to Cubby's to get a frozen cherry slush on a hot day. Even going to see one of my cousins was a hike. You haven't met Brandon yet, but trust me, there's only so much fun you can have on the ranch when you have to drag your little brother around with you everywhere."

Camilla laughed. "Well, I was the younger sibling getting dragged. Both my parents worked, so one of my brothers usually got stuck with me and Sofia. Instead of drawing straws, they'd shoot baskets. Felix usually lost."

"That's because Felix needs to lay off those three-pointers."

"Not when he has you rebounding them." She gave him a light kiss before getting out of the car.

The youth league game was already underway when they walked inside the stuffy gymnasium and headed toward the bleachers. Jordan didn't need to look for Mac on the opposite side of the hardwood court. Everyone could hear her since she was yelling way louder than anyone was cheering.

"Oh, no," Camilla said when they found some open seats.

"What's wrong?"

She pointed at her dad in the black-and-white-striped referee jersey using one of those wheeled knee walkers like a kid on a Razor scooter, zooming up and down the court as he weaved his way through the young players. "He promised my mom he wouldn't ref any more games until his doctor cleared him."

Mr. Sanchez stopped long enough to blow his whistle at Mac. "That's a warning, Coach. Watch the language from the sidelines. These are kids playing, not pros."

He zipped away on his knee scooter and Mac made a gesture at his back, which drew several gasps from the parents in the stands. Jordan scrubbed his hand over the lower half of his face to keep from laughing.

Camilla nodded toward the tall, thin woman on the green team's bench. The one with the blond ponytail, sporty yoga pants and sweatshirt printed with the words Team Work Makes the Dream Work. "Is that your assistant?"

Jordan closed his eyes and shook his head. "Nope."

"But I thought you said your assistant was coaching her first— Oh." Camilla giggled when her father blew his whistle again and Mac stomped onto the court arguing that her player didn't double dribble.

"Normally, she coaches baseball and softball." Jordan moved his hand up so that he could rub the left side of his temple where a tic was suddenly developing. "But her friend works for the parks department and asked her to sub today. Five bucks says they don't ask her back."

Surprisingly, Mac didn't get kicked out before halftime. After sending her players to get their water bottles, the older woman jogged over to the bleachers. "Whatcha doing here, Sport? You usually only come to my baseball games."

He tugged on his ear. "That's because the sound of you yelling at the umpires doesn't echo as much when you're on a grassy field instead of an enclosed gymnasium."

His assistant snorted. "Well, that ref is blind as a bat."

"Mac, allow me to introduce Camilla Sanchez, the blind bat's daughter."

"Pleasure to meet you." Mac stuck out her hand. "No offense about your old man."

"None taken." Camilla smiled as they shook hands. "Just between us, he actually enjoys it when coaches challenge him. Keeps him on his toes. Or at least half of his toes today."

"I like this one," Mac told Jordan. "She the one you had me put out my scouting report on?"

"Scouting report?" Camilla arched a brow. Jordan was now rubbing his entire forehead.

"Yep." Mac shoved an escaped wiry gray curl back under her ball cap. "After that fancy party, my boy here was all kinds of fired up wanting to find this mystery woman he met."

Camilla tilted her head as she studied him. "Is that so?"

"I think scouting report might be a bit of an overstatement." He lifted one shoulder, then dropped it. "I was just looking for a name and number."

Mac made a snorting sound, then leaned toward Camilla and stage-whispered, "Now I see why you have him swinging for the fences." She chuckled, then returned to her regular voice. "Gotta get back to my team and give them my words of wisdom for the second half. I'll catch you two after the game."

Camilla wiggled her eyebrows at him. "Now I can't wait to hear more."

"You know those relatives who like to bring out the baby book and say all sorts of stuff to embarrass you?" Jordan rolled his shoulders backward. "That's Mac."

Camilla glanced back and forth between him and his assistant on the opposite side of the court. "I didn't know that you're related."

"She's the closest thing I've got to a grandmother," he offered. "I guess you could say that since my mom left when I was younger, she really is the closest thing I have to a mom, too."

"How old were you when your parents divorced?" Camilla asked.

"Seven."

"Do you ever see her?"

"No. There was a pre-nup and she knew she wasn't going to get much in alimony, so she went the full custody route instead."

Camilla made a tsking sound. "You make it sound like the only reason she wanted custody was for the child support payments."

He crossed his arms in front of his chest and managed a shrug. But his jaw stayed tight.

"Jordan?" Camilla placed her hand between his shoulder blades. "Surely you don't think that your own mother didn't want you."

"It was the one time she stood up to my dad. Or rather her hired attorney stood up to him. She won custody and we lived with her for a whole month in a house my father bought. Turns out Cornelius only let her think she won because he knew what would eventually happen. He was just biding his time until he could buy her off. One weekend, she dropped us off at the ranch for a visit and didn't come back. My dad kept sending the child support checks, though, and she kept cashing them."

"I'm so sorry." Her hand made circles along his upper back. "I didn't think... I didn't know."

"It's okay." He swallowed, his throat thick with emotion. "There may be a lot of things I don't like about my father, but taking care of his children has always been his number one priority, no matter the cost."

Several minutes passed and neither one of them said a word. Which was a relief because Margaret Taylor was the last person he wanted to talk about. Camilla continued a rhythmic massaging motion until his muscles finally loosened.

"So tell me about this scouting report." She slid her hand from his back to loop through his arm and leaned into his side. "You really wanted to find me that badly, huh?"

"Mac has a big mouth. Especially for someone who wasn't that much help in my search."

He felt her vibrate with laughter, and Jordan realized there was no place else he would've rather been than sitting on a wooden bench inside a stuffy, overheated gymnasium watching a bunch of eight-year-olds he didn't know play a very unimpressive game of basketball.

When he was with Camilla, though, everything was an experience.

Camilla knew her dad had to have seen them in the stands since the gymnasium wasn't even a third of the way filled. But even after the final buzzer, he kept his back to the bleachers, probably to keep from making eye contact with her.

So she and Jordan waited for him by the exit.

"Does Mom know you're here?" she asked when her father realized he wasn't going to be able to roll by them on his knee scooter. "You didn't drive yourself, did you?"

"No, Dylan brought me and loaned me his referee jersey since your mother hid both of mine." Her dad turned to Jordan and shook his hand before adding, "And now you're both accomplices because you stayed and watched without stopping me. Let me change out of this shirt and then you guys can give me a ride back to the house."

"Hey, I'm staying out of it." Jordan put up both of his hands. "I've got an appointment with Mrs. Sanchez on Wednesday and I'm not about to lie to the woman who has the power to give me a bowl-shaped haircut."

"Don't worry. Mom's clients are a walking advertisement for her shop. She wouldn't want Jordan—" Camilla caught herself before saying his last name in front of her dad. "She wouldn't want *you* looking like you got a bad haircut."

Jordan tilted his head and lifted an eyebrow, as though he knew she was avoiding telling her father who he really was.

"Don't look now." Her dad maneuvered himself closer between Camilla and Jordan, as though he was pulling them into a huddle. "That crazy coach is heading this way."

"Dad, that crazy coach is Jordan's...friend." Camilla wasn't quite sure how to explain who Mac was. She didn't want to say "employee" or even "coworker" because clearly the woman was special to him. But she also didn't want to bring up the earlier conversation about Jordan's mother.

"Good game, Ref," Mac said when she approached the group.

"That's not what you said in the third quarter," her father challenged, but grudgingly shook the older woman's hand.

"You mean after you blew that whistle in my face and said I needed to stick to baseball and leave basketball to the real athletes?"

"Dad," Camilla scolded her father. "Sorry, Mac. My family is a little obsessed with their favorite sport."

"Nothing wrong with having a little passion for something." Jordan's assistant nudged him. "Right, sport?"

"Why do I get the feeling that you're suggesting I don't get passionate, Mac?" Jordan asked, almost daring the woman to announce the answer to everyone.

And she didn't disappoint.

"Well, you used to love football. But after college, the only thing you seem to be passionate about is not getting passionate about anything." Mac turned to Camilla and gave her a bold wink. "At least until now."

Camilla felt the heat rising from the depths of her chest to the roots of her hair. Jordan's own cheeks were a charming shade of pink, but his smile directed at Camilla seemed to say, *See. I told you that you were different.* It was almost as though he'd known exactly what Mac would say and purposely set up the question to prove his point.

"Oh, hell," her dad said, clearly oblivious to Camilla and Jordan making googly eyes at each other right there under the digital scoreboard. Instead, he was using his scooter to kneel down lower between them. "Speaking of passionate, here comes your mother. How did she find out I was here?"

"Aaron Sanchez," Denise called as she strode into the gymnasium. "Stop hiding behind our daughter and face me like a real man."

Mac made a snickering sound, but Jordan's eyes grew wide. Camilla thought about their earlier conversation about Jessica's interaction with Cornelius and the most recent revelation about his own mother so easily giving him up. She wondered when Jordan had last seen a wife stand up to her husband. Again she slipped her arm through his and whispered, "Don't worry."

"Hermosa!" Dad used the term of endearment that always got him off the hook with his wife. "Your hair looks beautiful. Is that a new color?"

Mom touched her freshly straightened mahogany bangs briefly—she was always experimenting with different styles and colors and appreciated it when people noticed—then quickly pointed an accusing finger at her husband. "Don't you *hermosa* me, Aaron. The doctor said no physical activity for six weeks. Do you want to make your foot worse?"

Dad took a dramatic breath, his mouth practically pouting beneath his beard. "But you don't know what it's like to be stuck on the couch while everyone else gets to run around the court."

"Oh, if you want to get off the couch, I'll give you something to do. You can start by cleaning out that garage like you promised. Then you can paint that back bedroom…" Mom's voice trailed off with a list of household chores as Dad rolled behind her toward the exit.

The muscles in Jordan's arm relaxed and he whispered under his breath, "Well, at least she didn't get mad at us."

Camilla's mom turned around at that exact

second and pointed the same accusing finger at them. "And don't think you guys are off the hook for not stopping him or calling me. You two are both on kitchen duty tonight, so you better stop by the market on your way over."

"Looks like I'm invited for dinner again." Jordan lifted one side of his mouth. Camilla pinched the bridge of her nose and didn't see his head dip close to hers until his lips brushed her ear. "And before you say it, it doesn't count as one of my dates if your mom invites me."

Chapter Seven

Early the following Wednesday morning, Jordan reminded himself that he was only making this uncomfortable sacrifice to impress Camilla. Then he pulled open one of etched glass double doors and cautiously entered the shop.

Inside, tranquil music played over the discreetly located speakers in the ceiling and displays of fancy beauty products and expensive candles lined the shelves along the walls. The floor-to-ceiling water feature behind the empty receptionist desk was made of teak wood and stacked river rocks, and he had to peek around it to see Mrs. Sanchez waving him over to her station.

As he approached, she whipped the black cape off the back of her padded leather chair with a dramatic flourish, smiled warmly and said, "You're the calm before the storm."

Mrs. Sanchez must have seen him pause in hesitation, because she clarified, "That means you're my first appointment of the day. In about thirty minutes, it'll be packed in here."

"Oh." He resisted the urge to tug at his collar. Jordan couldn't remember the last time he'd been in a place like this. Probably not since he was a kid and his first stepmother, Tania, took him and his half brothers to a high-priced salon in Billings.

Wow. That wasn't a memory he'd thought about in quite some time. He hadn't even seen the twins, who were a little younger than Daphne, since Cornelius's divorce from their mother. Dirk and Dustin were the only Taylor offspring in several generations to not grow up on the ranch, yet Jordan still kept in contact with them to ensure they had everything they needed. Or at least Mac did and then reported back to him.

"Where do you normally go to get your cuts?" Mrs. Sanchez interrupted his thoughts as she lifted and inspected several chunks of his hair through her sparkle-studded reading glasses. She'd asked him several times to call her Denise, but Jordan still thought of her as Mrs. Sanchez.

"Uh, actually, there's a guy who comes to my office every few weeks." He didn't say that Jenkins was his father's longtime barber who often squeezed Jordan in after Cornelius's routine cuts. "It's just easier for my schedule that way."

"Hmm" was all Mrs. Sanchez offered in response. However, her downturned lips said plenty. She was not a fan of either his barber or his classic, but rumpled hairstyle.

The stainless steel table stationed beside her looked like a surgical tray, the tools of her trade strategically laid out. She picked up an angled comb and powered on her electric clippers.

She'd only finished the left side above his ear when the shop door opened again and a heavyset older woman bustled around the reception desk with a folded newspaper under one arm and a Pomeranian under the other. "Denise, my sister-in-law over in Rust Creek Falls just sent me a copy of last week's *Gazette*, and it has the most unbelievable story."

Mrs. Sanchez pointed the comb at the newcomer. "Mrs. Waters, if the health inspector shows up and sees Peanut Pie in my salon, you're paying the fine."

Jordan immediately recognized the name. Mrs. Waters was the next-door neighbor who'd brought over the bad casserole when Mr. Sanchez had his bunion surgery. Seizing on an opportunity to gather some additional insight about Camilla, Jordan tried to smile at the approaching woman whose short, tightly curled hair was so silver it was nearly blue. But Mrs. Sanchez forced his head forward so she could keep working.

"You said the same thing on Sunday, Denise." Mrs. Waters made a tsking sound. "But poor Peanut Pie's asthma is still acting up with all that chemical smell lingering in my house and it's too cold for me to leave the windows open while I'm gone."

"If you would lay off the home perms, Mrs. Waters, then Peanut Pie—and the rest of us—would all breathe a lot easier."

"Anyway, do you want to hear my story or not?" The plump woman in a snug orange velour track suit plopped herself and Peanut Pie into the empty salon chair next to them and unfolded the newspaper.

Unfortunately, Jordan couldn't see much of what Mrs. Waters was showing them. If he so much as tilted his head, he'd risk Mrs. Sanchez nipping him with the clippers. Due to all the buzzing around his ears, he also missed several parts of the story. From what he could pick up, though, there was some secret baby put up for adoption seventy-five years ago over in Rust Creek Falls. Apparently, everyone across the entire state of Montana was following the story of this family's search because it had something to do with a famous psychic named Winona. There was a lead that the baby might've been named Beatrix but now went by the name Daisy. Or maybe it was Stacy? Now Mrs. Waters was singing a song about daisies. Yep. The name was definitely Daisy.

When Mrs. Sanchez traded out the electric clippers for a very sharp pair of scissors, Jordan quickly raised his head to the large mirror on the wall, only to find Mrs. Waters's eager eyes making direct contact with his. "Have you heard anything?"

Jordan slowly glanced around the shop to see who the woman was talking to. He could hear somebody on the other side of the receptionist desk asking about something called a seaweed hydration pedicure and another hairdresser was now at the shampoo bowl with a customer and clearly out of earshot. He lifted a brow and asked, "Heard anything about what?"

"About the secret baby. Rumor is that the Abernathys are involved and I figured you would know more since you live by them, Mr. Taylor."

Jordan jerked his head up and heard Mrs. Sanchez mutter a curse. "Keep still, *mijo*, or it's going to be lopsided."

He recognized the Spanish term of endearment, which made him hope that Camilla's mom was so focused on what she was doing, she hadn't heard Mrs. Waters's use of his last name. Forcing his shoulders to relax, he smiled wide at the Sanchezes' neighbor. "Please, call me Jordan. Mister sounds like you're talking to my father."

Mrs. Waters snorted. "As if anyone would mistake you for that flashy blowhard Cornelius Taylor."

Jordan's lungs paused midbreath right as the scissors poised above his scalp paused midclip. So much for hoping. Using the reflection of the mirror, he searched the face of Mrs. Sanchez, who was standing behind him. Instead of shooting daggers at him, she kept her eyes directed at the wet brown hair measured between her fingers and murmured, "Not that anyone could tell the difference judging by your duplicate hairstyles."

Thankfully, a third stylist had arrived and called the older woman over to the shampoo bowl right then and Mrs. Sanchez returned to her diligent cutting.

He should have been relieved she wasn't kicking Jordan out of the shop halfway through his haircut. After all, given Mrs. Waters's reference to his father being a flashy blowhard, it was perfectly clear how the citizens of Bronco Valley felt about his family. Now he understood why Camilla had warned him about telling the Sanchezes who he was.

Still.

Jordan couldn't just sit here like a coward, as though he had something to hide. When he finally caught Mrs. Sanchez's eyes in the mirror he said, "So, now you know."

She set the scissors down and ran the comb through his hair a few more times, as though she needed a moment to think of her response. Jordan's heart pounded as his mind rushed through several defenses and explanations. Yet he shouldn't have to apologize for who he was or where he was raised any more than Camilla should. He straightened his shoulders under the black stylist's cape.

Finally, she sighed and said, "I knew all along, *mijo*. Nobody in this town is better informed on all the local gossip—including your unfortunate nicknames—than I am. Not only did I help Camilla get ready for her big night at that fundraiser gala at your place, I spent the following week with most of my clients showing me the pictures of her online."

"So does everyone else know?" he asked hopefully. It would make everything so much easier if he and Camilla could just date openly.

"Let's hope not," she replied a bit too quickly,

and Jordan's optimism immediately deflated. "I saw you in the background of one of those pictures, you know. At the fundraiser. You were far enough away from her that nobody had put two and two together yet. But I saw the way you were looking at my daughter and I knew what was coming well before you showed up at our house."

Mrs. Sanchez spread some pomade on her hands before applying it to his hair, which he had to admit looked about ten times better than when his father's barber did it. Jordan wouldn't be satisfied with just a trendy hairstyle, though. He wanted Camilla's mom's blessing.

Or at least her acceptance.

"So you're okay with your daughter dating the so-called Charmed Prince of Bronco Heights?" Jordan inwardly cringed even as he continued to force out the hated words. "The Rancher Most Wanted?"

"Just don't bring it up to anyone else." Mrs. Sanchez whipped the cape off him with finality. "They might not understand what Camilla sees in you."

Jordan left the salon with, he had to admit, the best-looking haircut he'd ever had, as well as a ball of confusion cranking through his gut. Still, he told himself to focus on the positive. Namely, that Camilla did in fact see something in him and her mother clearly understood what that was. Mrs. Sanchez had even called him *mijo* a second time. He should at least be comforted by that, right?

Instead, all he could think about was the looming fact that the rest of her family might never accept him.

Jordan took Denise Sanchez's advice to heart and didn't say a word to the rest of the family about being a Taylor, which was trickier to do since he was more comfortable spending time with the Sanchezes than he was with his own family.

There were a few times when he'd wanted to proudly claim his heritage. But then there were the times when he just sat back and listened. Especially when Dante made a comment about his students in the Bronco Unified School District not having enough funding from the state because many of the wealthier citizens from the Heights were sending their children to posh private schools.

As long as the rest of the Sanchez family didn't associate him with some of his neighbors, Jordan grew more confident that their open invitation to Sunday night dinners would last indefinitely. Not only was it entertaining to watch them playfully argue and push each other's buttons, but being around them was a bonus to spending time with Camilla.

And considering the fact that Camilla was as active in her community as she was at work and school, the free time she *did* have to spend with Jordan was very limited. In fact, he soon learned that the best way to be around her—and not have it count as a date—was when he found out where she would be ahead of time and "accidentally" ran into her there. Never at work, though, since that would've just made things more awkward. He was now well aware of the social power imbalance between them, so having her wait on him as a customer at the restaurant would've made both of them uncomfortable.

Instead, by strategically fitting himself into her busy life, he could prove to her, and everyone else, that he was taking this seriously. By the middle of November, Jordan had already participated in a creek-side cleanup, a coat drive and a Cub Scout car wash (Mr. Sanchez, the troop leader, couldn't risk getting his surgery incision wet, so his daughter filled in). All of this, just so he could be around Camilla.

Hell, he'd volunteered so much lately, he would've been in danger of losing his own job if he wasn't already in line to inherit a share of the company.

A fact that Cornelius reminded him of a week later.

"You seem to be spending a lot of time away from the office lately," his father said at breakfast on Saturday morning. "I don't suppose that has anything to do with you seeing that girl."

"As a matter of fact, it does." Jordan didn't take a seat at the formal dining table because he had no intention of staying here long. "Her name is Camilla and I'm so glad you encouraged me to talk to her at the gala."

Cornelius's nostrils flared. "Don't try and turn this around on me, young man. At the time, I was under the impression she was a Balthazar."

"Well, your mistake helped me get my foot in the door with her so I'm grateful to you all the same. Things are going very well between Camilla and me, so I'd suggest you choose your next words very carefully."

Clearly, Cornelius knew by now that arguing with his oldest son was like a chess match, one he didn't want to lose. Instead of going after Camilla, his father stared at him for several moments, his silver eyebrows drawn together in an angry crease, before shifting tactics. "Is that another new shirt from one of your latest pet projects?"

Jordan glanced at the green Bronco Valley Rec Center tee. Somehow, he'd gotten roped into coaching the girls' basketball team after they'd asked Mac not to return. "It is. But don't worry, Dad. I'm still clocking in plenty of hours at Taylor Beef."

Which was true. In the evenings when Camilla was working at DJ's Deluxe, Jordan would return to his own office and catch up on reports and usually a stack of papers Mac left for him to sign.

"Speaking of beef." Cornelius waved away the fresh fruit and Greek yogurt parfait Jessica requested the private chef to make. "Is it too much for a man to get some steak and eggs around here?"

"But the doctor told you that you need to be cutting back on the red meat, and I thought this might…um…." Jessica looked at Jordan, her wide eyes silently pleading for some backup.

Everyone always turned to Jordan when they needed backup dealing with Cornelius.

Jordan hadn't been exaggerating when he'd told Camilla that his nickname at work was the Smoother. Unfortunately, he was usually called in to smooth things over with his stubborn old man. Cornelius Taylor's biggest fear in life was having someone think he was weak. The guy hadn't always been this way, especially when his kids were younger. But each time something in life didn't go his way—a divorce, a bad investment deal, a daughter who didn't want to go into the family business—Cornelius would double down on his efforts to be in control of his image. Or, at least what he thought his image should be.

Jordan sighed. "It's not going to kill you to eat a little healthier, Dad. Yogurt comes from cows, so nobody will think any less of you."

"This is how it started with your sister, you know." His father pointed a spoon at Jordan, and at first he thought he was only going to have to hear a rant about Daphne's food choices. No such luck. "Volunteering *once in a while* is fine, Jordan. But do you have to give up all your valuable time to these charities? You already have commitments at work and commitments to this family. Just do what I do and send a check."

"I'll keep that in mind." Jordan reached for an apple out of the fruit bowl in the center of the table. Now wasn't the time to disagree with his father because Cornelius was currently digging into his yogurt parfait and to start an argument would only serve as a distraction. It was better to pick his battles.

Or in this case, Jessica's battle, who mouthed the words *thank you* to Jordan before he headed into the kitchen to find the loaded breakfast burrito she'd had the chef wrap up for him.

Sure, Jordan might be burning the candle at both ends lately, eating most of his meals either in his car or in his office. In fact, he was exhausted by the time he fell into bed every night. But it was well worth it.

First, he was getting to know Camilla on her home turf, where she felt free to be herself. Although, if he was being honest, she was pretty damn authentic no matter where she was or who she was with. Even in a borrowed gown at a black tie gala or on the back of a thousand-pound Arabian stallion, her infectious laugh and zest for life stood out above all else.

Second, he was actually getting involved with the community again. He hadn't felt this connected to his hometown since he'd played football at Bronco High. Third, and most important, by fitting himself into her life, he was buying himself more time in Camilla's presence.

After all, their agreement never specified that the three weeks needed to be concurrent. It was a win-win as far as he was concerned because he still had those guaranteed dates sitting in his back pocket.

One downside to volunteering so often, though, was that no matter where he ended up, there was usually a news story or a social media post with a picture of him there. Camilla took great pains to avoid being caught anywhere near him in the photos since the comment sections were always littered with speculations about Jordan's newfound interest in community events.

The other downside was that since none of those events counted as actual dates and usually took place in public, he'd now gone a couple weeks without kissing Camilla.

Finally, on a Sunday afternoon before Thanksgiving, they had their fourth date. Albeit, it wasn't the most romantic place Jordan would've taken her.

"How much money do you think they waste on samples?" he asked Camilla as they turned down another aisle in some big box warehouse store near Billings.

"It's not really a waste if they end up selling more product because people enjoy the samples," she countered.

"But all these people are just grabbing the samples without actually putting the item in their carts. It'd be interesting to see a cost analysis report on it."

Camilla took a tiny paper cup filled with cornbread stuffing from a tray. "For the past thirty plus years, this company has been giving away free samples in thousands of stores all across the globe. I'm pretty sure they're still coming out on top."

"Are you planning on following that same business model when you open your restaurant?" Jordan took the last sample cup of stuffing from the tray before an employee set out another batch. "I don't know if potential investors will be on board with that."

"They already are." Camilla smiled at Jordan.

"Wait." He stopped in the center of the aisle, and an older woman riding in an electric scooter behind him clipped his boot heels as she swung around to avoid him. "You already found an investor?"

"Yep. We signed the contracts two days ago."

"Who is it?"

"They're a silent partner, so I'm not allowed to say." Camilla avoided eye contact with him by scanning her grocery list. "I think the canned green beans are down here."

"Are you sure your mom wants canned beans?" Jordan asked as he pushed the oversized shopping cart behind her. "I've eaten with your family several times now and everything is always fresh. Thanks to Mr. Granada." See, he was even in on the family jokes about the store clerk who had a crush on Mrs. Sanchez.

"My parents insist. When they moved here thirty years ago and celebrated their first Thanksgiving, Mrs. Waters gave them all these recipes for what she called 'traditional American dishes.'" Camilla held up two fingers on each hand to simulate air quotes. "Mom was pregnant with Dylan and on bed rest so my dad cooked everything himself, including the green bean casserole. Later on, they learned that there were much better recipes out there. But at the time it was their way of embracing the culture of their new country. Now, it's a reminder of all the challenges they've had to overcome since they became citizens. It's not Thanksgiving at our house without Mrs. Waters's recipes."

Jordan hefted a huge box of green beans into the cart. "Your brothers are big guys, but there's no way they're going to eat all of these."

"No, but there's a food pantry at the church and we usually give half to them ahead of time."

They were standing in front of crates of twenty-pound sacks of potatoes when Jordan tried again. "So how did you meet this investor?"

"I can't say." Camilla shrugged as she gazed longingly at the red fingerlings and the Yukon golds.

"You can't? Or you won't?" he asked, the disappointment of a missed opportunity threading through him. Despite how much he wanted to be her partner, he obviously couldn't continue his personal relationship with Camilla if he went into business with her. For one, he didn't ever want her to feel indebted to him. For another, those kinds of ventures never ended well when the parties decided to part socially. However, he'd actually talked to several of his associates who were interested in meeting with her and finding out more about her restaurant.

Camilla made a zipper motion in front of her lips, then pretended to lock them shut and throw away the key.

"It sounds shady," he finally said.

"What does?" She went with the standard russets and didn't even budge under the weight as she put the bag in the cart.

"This mysterious silent partner. Why do they want to keep it a secret? Do they not want people to know they're investing in you?"

"Jordan, I assure you that it's all on the up and up. And not *those* yams. We need to go back to the canned section for them. Do you think the marshmallows would be with the baking products or in the candy section?"

"I'm pretty sure I saw marshmallows on that display stand by the pie crusts." He put the smaller bag back, already feeling his insulin levels spike at the thought of what Mrs. Waters put in her sweet potato casserole. "What if this mystery investor is trying to take advantage of you?"

"Because I'm not business savvy enough to know better?" She crossed her arms in front of her chest, but a mom with three kids hanging off the sides of her shopping cart needed to maneuver by. Camilla's stance lost some of its defiance as she was forced to squeeze herself against the red onions. Yet that didn't detract from her argument. "Suppose I made a big mistake, Jordan? What would you do? Rush in to save me?"

"You know I didn't mean it that way," he said as he followed her down the next aisle.

"How do I know what you mean? I barely know you at all."

"Oh, come on, Camilla." The cart was getting surprisingly more full and harder to steer by the time they got out of the produce section. "By now you probably know me better than anyone else does. Besides maybe Daphne and Mac."

"And you should know that when it comes to you, I'm always going to protect myself." She held up one palm as though the hand gesture was enough to stop his train of thought. "Not that I think you would intentionally hurt me. But what happens after our three weeks are up? What happens after three months? Eventually you'll move on to the next shiny object."

"That's not fair." He leaned his forearms on the cart, not moving until she realized she was prematurely judging him. Again.

"Oh, yeah? What has been your longest relationship?" She put her hands on her waist, drawing his attention to the spot below, where her snug jeans hugged her hips.

His mouth went dry and he looked around

for a sample cart offering water or juice or even Scotch if they had it. "That depends on how you define relationship."

"You shouldn't have to define it, Jordan. You should know when you're in a relationship."

"In that case, this one has been the longest."

"This one?" She peered around him at the pallets of cereal as though there were another relationship lurking behind them. "The one between me and you?"

"If I'm defining what a relationship is, then I'd say this qualifies."

"Four dates isn't enough time to define anything," she replied.

"Here's how I see it. I've never done Sunday dinners with a woman's family. I've never volunteered for community service projects just to be around a woman. I've never let a woman ride one of my favorite horses. Don't tell Leia I said Palp was one of my favorites, by the way. She thinks she's my only one."

"Aha!" Camilla pointed a finger at his chest. "How many other females out there think they're your only one?"

"None! Because I've never done any of this with another woman." Jordan dashed a frustrated hand through his hair before he continued. "I *certainly* have never gone grocery shopping with one and gotten into an argument with her in the middle of the breakfast aisle. But what should be even more telling is that I've never wanted to *keep* doing those things with anyone else but you. Therefore, the fact that I want to be with you, along with the fact that you clearly want to be with me, makes this, by default, a relationship."

She studied him for several seconds, but he could see her breathing had quickened because her red puffy vest was straining against her breasts. Finally she asked, "How do you know I want to be with you?"

"Because you're not the kind of person who wastes time. You go after what you want." He took a step closer and, as though to prove his point, she didn't retreat. "If you didn't want to be with me, you never would have agreed to this three-week trial. If you weren't attracted to me, you wouldn't let me touch you like this." He reached out to trail his hand along her waist under her vest, and when her full lips parted in surprise, he lowered his head and his voice. "You most definitely wouldn't let me kiss you in the middle of a crowded store."

His mouth hovered above hers until she grabbed a fistful of his shirt and pulled him against her. Camilla's kisses were better than breathing. Jordan's lungs filled with the intoxicating scent of her lavender shampoo, and his hands filled with the intoxicating feel of her rear end as he hauled her hips against his. She moaned and…

Something else was ringing in his ears. He pulled back when he heard a second metal clang.

An aproned employee held a stainless steel spoon over her portable stove as she frowned at them. "You kids need to go do that hanky-panky stuff somewhere else. You're blocking my oatmeal samples."

Chapter Eight

For the past couple of weeks, Camilla had done her best to show Jordan how the other half lived in a fruitless attempt to prove that their lifestyles were incompatible. Surprisingly, though, the stubborn man seemed game for whatever she'd dished up. And he kept coming back for more.

He'd even gone grocery shopping yesterday at the big box store an hour out of town just so he could be with her. Other than that steamy kiss in the breakfast aisle, there was nothing romantic about their $1.50 hot dogs and sodas in the food court or those countless samples they'd filled up on.

Yet Jordan seemed to enjoy every second of whatever random errand or service project she had on her schedule, which only made Camilla question whether she'd been wrong about him all along. In fact, the more involved he got in the Bronco Valley community, the more Camilla felt her resolve slipping.

And don't even get her started on her family. They all adored him, even Dylan, who hadn't been too pleased to find out that Jordan's favorite NBA player was on the team of his sworn rivals.

Of course, none of the Sanchezes knew that he was one of *those* Taylors.

So far, the only thing Camilla had proven to anyone was that her and Jordan's physical attraction was only growing stronger. Maybe she needed to get him back in his own world to show him that *she* was the one who wouldn't be able to fit in. That would be easy enough to do with his dad and stepmother. Maybe even his siblings.

DJ's Deluxe was doing a limited menu this week due to all the Thanksgiving holiday takeout orders, which meant she wasn't working her usual shifts. Plus, she'd booked a couple of vacation days to be able to spend time cooking with her parents—and, of course, to spend time with Jordan. And since school was on break, she didn't have any online lectures or reading assignments. So when Jordan texted her that morning asking if they could have another "official date," she replied, I want to meet the rest of your family.

Camilla had anticipated a formal dinner at the Taylor estate prepared by a classically trained private chef and served by a stiff-lipped butler. Or perhaps another helicopter ride to a five-star restaurant in Jackson Hole. At this point, she wouldn't have been surprised if he'd pulled out the big guns and hired a private jet to ferry them to some romantic European city.

What she hadn't anticipated, she realized as they pulled up under the wooden sign of Happy Hearts Animal Sanctuary on Monday afternoon, was that he would take her to meet the other member of the Taylor family who didn't quite fit in, either.

"Jordan!" His sister nearly squealed as she ran over to hug her brother. "What are you doing away from the office? You never take time off from work... Oh." The pretty strawberry blonde trailed off when she caught sight of Camilla. "This is certainly a first on so many levels."

"Daph, this is Camilla Sanchez. Remember, I told you all about her?"

"I see my very determined and slightly stubborn brother finally found his mystery woman from the ball." Jordan's sister shot him a knowing smile before extending a hand to Camilla. "I'm Daphne Taylor."

"Nice to meet you," she replied. After a few more knowing looks passed between Jordan and Daphne, Camilla asked, "So does everyone in your family know the story of how Jordan and I met?"

"Only those of us who pay attention. Although I have to admit that I thought this particular quest would end up as another lost cause."

Something knotted in Camilla's throat at that admission, but she held her smile in place. Or tried to, but Daphne must've read her mind. "Not that I'm not happy to be proven wrong. It's just that I know how my brother is. Clearly, from what I've heard around town, though, you're not just a flavor of the month."

Camilla suddenly wanted to know what else Daphne had heard around town. But she turned to Jordan instead and didn't bother to hide her sarcasm. "Hmmm. Why does it always feel as though people are surprised when they find out we've had more than a couple of dates? It's almost as though they know your reputation."

Daphne chuckled. "It's hard *not* to know about his reputation, considering everyone reads about it online."

"You guys should understand by now that I'm not as bad as they make me out to be." Jordan dug his hands in the back pockets of his black slacks. He'd obviously come straight from his office to pick her up. Daphne's words about her brother never taking time off work repeated in Camilla's head. Maybe she was truly different from the other women he'd dated. "Besides, can't a man bring his favorite girl to meet his favorite sister without everyone bringing up his past?"

"You're right. My brother almost never visits his favorite sister. And certainly not with his girlfriend. Come on." Daphne moved between them and looped her arms through theirs. "Let me give you a tour of my farm."

Jordan's sister talked eagerly about each of the rescued animals at Happy Hearts, and Camilla tried to pay attention. But she couldn't stop thinking about how easily Daphne had referred to her as Jordan's girlfriend.

"As you can see," Daphne said as they got to an enclosed area near the end of the barn, "Happy Hearts is quite smaller than the Taylor Ranch and runs at a fraction of the cost—mostly raised through donations."

"Who's this big guy?" Jordan asked, making Camilla look inside the pen.

"That's Tiny Tim," Daphne replied. The pot-bellied pig was anything but tiny. "He came to live with us after his owner passed away."

The pig stuck its snout through the slats in the

fencing and sniffed Camilla's hand. She looked at Daphne for permission. "Is it okay if I pet him?"

"Sure." Daphne unlatched the gate. "You can even go inside and play with him. He's house-broken and actually knows quite a few tricks. In fact, that muddy wad of strings and patches used to be a soccer ball, and he'll kick it back to you if you roll it to him."

Camilla rolled the ball several times and the pig actually used a front hoof to kick it back. She bent over to retrieve the ball, and Tim pushed his snout into her palm. Camilla knelt in the straw to stroke the silky space between his ears and he oinked in appreciation. "Oh, he's an absolute sweetheart."

"You can say that again. In fact, he's a real charmer. All the females around here love him. Even old Agatha, the crankiest goat you'll ever meet. In fact, he's such a ladies' man, we thought about changing his name to—"

"Don't say it." Jordan shook his head at his sister.

Daphne laughed. "I was going to say Casanova. But now that you suggest it, Jordan Junior would've been just as appropriate."

"The ladies may love us," Jordan said to the pig, "but they certainly don't understand us."

Tim oinked in agreement.

"So what'll happen to him?" Camilla asked.

"My guess is as good as yours," Daphne replied, staring at her brother, who in turn was watching Camilla. "I've never seen him this smitten with a woman before."

"She's talking about the pig," Jordan said. "Not me."

"Oh." Daphne straightened. "We'll try to find him a good home. Otherwise, he will spend the rest of his days here at Happy Hearts, eating slop and lounging in the mud and charming all the females."

"Sounds like a pretty good life, if you ask me." Jordan knelt beside her. "I mean, except for the part about charming all the females. There's only one female I want to impress."

"I wish I could take you home, boy." Camilla continued to scratch the pig's head, refusing to acknowledge Jordan's comment for fear she'd turn as pink as Tim. "But I only have a studio apartment and absolutely no free time to speak of."

"Is she still talking about the pig?" Daphne laughed. "Because I already like any woman who can tell one of the Taylor men no."

"Then you'll love Camilla." Jordan winked at Daphne. "She has no problem telling me no."

A truck backed up close to the barn doors. Daphne sighed. "That's the second delivery of grain this week for the horses. I better help un-load it."

"I've got it, Daph," Jordan offered, easily swinging himself over the wood slatted fence. "You already do too much around here as it is."

He left the two women standing in the pig pen together, and Camilla knew what was coming before Daphne even opened her mouth. "Well, you've certainly succeeded with my brother where many others before you have failed."

"Don't get your hopes up," Camilla said more to herself than to Jordan's sister. "I'm sure it's only temporary. He'll lose interest soon enough."

"I don't know. When Jordan makes up his mind, it's pretty hard to convince him to change it."

Camilla tilted her head as she watched Jordan, clad in his business attire, hop into the back of a pickup truck to unload heavy burlap sacks. "He certainly is determined. I have a feeling that's what attracted him to me in the first place. The challenge."

"I'm the first to admit that my brother is used to getting his way." Daphne nodded. "In fact, I even accused him of being just like our father when he was trying to find you. I was so an-noyed with him, I told him I wouldn't help. I was worried that he was envisioning you as some sort of prize that he needed to win. But seeing him with you is different."

Camilla's emotions were so damn twisted and tangled. She wanted to be flattered that what they potentially had was something special. But it also made her more wary that it might get messy when the three-week trial dating was up. And the fact remained that it would be up soon. Steeling herself, she asked the question she might not want to know the answer to. "How so?"

"The way he looks at you. The way he laughs when you confront him. All of our lives, we've witnessed people bend over backward to accommodate our father. Fawning over him and telling him whatever he wanted to hear. When women started to do that to Jordan, he would get all cagey and cut them loose. We've all teased him about his dating history, but I'm starting to realize that the real reason he hasn't wanted to settle down is that he *doesn't* want to end up like Cornelius Taylor."

"If being like your dad is such a concern for him, why does Jordan still work for the family business? Why does he still live at home?" Camilla didn't have any experience with the man other than that day he called her by the wrong name. But Jordan didn't seem anything like their father.

"Because Jordan loves a challenge. And, in

a way, he also feels sorry for our father and thinks he can fix things. Jordan seems to think the reason our dad can be so controlling and overbearing with us kids is because deep down, he's afraid he's going to lose us. When I decided to move off the ranch to open my own farm, you would've thought I told our father that I was leaving the family for good. Who knows? Maybe it reminded him of when our mom left. All I knew was that the harder my dad tried to get me to stay, the more I needed to get out of there. Jordan, though, is the opposite. He thinks he can change my dad's flaws by working on things from the inside. And maybe he can someday. Did I mention that my brother is very stubborn and determined?"

Camilla sighed. "He's definitely determined to prove that we're right for each other."

"From what I've seen so far today, not to mention what I've read on social media about his sudden interest in volunteering, there's no question that you're the right woman for him."

Unfortunately, that didn't mean Jordan was the right man for her. Which meant that Camilla's conflicting emotions made her feel as though she was right back at square one.

Camilla cast several furtive looks Jordan's way on the drive home from Happy Hearts.

She'd seen him tired, wound up and even slightly defensive. But she'd yet to see the man in a bad mood, even when one of the grain sacks tore open as he was carrying it on his shoulder and spilled oat pellets all over his designer suit. She'd certainly never seen him as quiet as he was right now.

So when he'd barely said more than a few sentences by the time they were driving down the main street of Bronco Valley, Camilla knew something must be weighing heavily on his mind. Maybe one of Daphne's comments had gotten under his skin and now he was having second thoughts about finishing out their final week of dates.

An empty pit slowly formed in Camilla's stomach as she thought about Jordan changing his mind so quickly. Mentally, she'd been preparing herself for it all along, but now that it was about to happen, her body wasn't ready for it.

By the time he pulled into the side alley parking spot beneath her apartment, her elbow was braced on the leather armrest of the passenger side door, her fingers clenching the handle so she could quickly dive out of the car to get away from the inevitable awkward conversation.

"So, thanks for the ride," she started, gathering the handles of her purse in her free hand so she could bolt.

"Camilla, before we get out, I've been thinking about something the whole way here and I want to just get it out in the open now." He turned toward her, and that empty pit in her belly suddenly felt like a ton of bricks. His expression was somber without so much as a hint of a smirk or the creasing of a dimple as he continued. "I know we agreed on three weeks. But…"

Yep. Her entire insides went all achy as he looked up at the sunroof, as though he was trying to find the right words to dump her. "But…?" she prompted.

He opened his mouth and she thought, *Here it is.* "But I'm already done for."

"So you're ready to call it quits." She nodded in acceptance, swallowing her own disappointment.

"No!" His brown eyes widened as he jerked his head back in surprise. Then he reached across the center console to take her hand in his. He had to practically pry her fingers from the death grip on her purse. "I mean I don't need three weeks."

"But we haven't even slept together yet." Camilla nearly slammed her palm over her mouth. She hadn't meant to say that out loud, but she'd thought that if Jordan were going to break up with her, he'd likely wait until after he'd gotten the ultimate prize. "Not that I'm trying to get you in bed or anything. I just figured that you wouldn't give up before you, uh, sealed the deal."

"Who says I'm giving up?" he asked.

She tried to ignore the way his fingers were now interlaced with hers. The way his thumb was slowly stroking the soft pad of her palm. "But you just told me you don't need to spend any more time with me."

"No, I'm saying that I don't need another minute to know how I feel. I have totally and completely fallen for you." His admission shot a rush of adrenaline through Camilla, and her brain went all topsy-turvy. Before she could ask him if he was serious, those playful dimples returned and he brought the back of her hand up to his mouth. "Of course, I *am* more than willing to sleep together, if that's what it'll take to convince you."

When his lips caressed her knuckles like that, all she could think about was every other spot on her body she wanted him to kiss.

"It's just that it's probably too soon for us to be taking things to that level," she said. Sparks flew through her nerve endings as his teeth scraped against the inside of her wrist. She lost her train of thought as she stared at his very capable mouth.

His eyes stayed focused on what he was doing,

his lips brushing against her skin as he spoke. "It kind of feels like we're already at that level."

"There's just so much we don't know about each…aw, hell." She cupped his jaw with her free hand and lifted his face to hers for a kiss. It was cold outside, the first hints of snowfall dusting his windshield, but her skin felt as though she could melt an arctic freeze. She was hot and flushed and nearly throbbing with need as they fought against the center console to get closer to each other. When Jordan broke the kiss, she heard a whimpering sound and realized it came from her.

The windows were steamed with the fog of their heavy breathing as they stared at each other, both of them dazed from another heat-filled kiss.

Jordan was the first to break the silence. "I want to do this, Camilla. You have no idea how much I've been wanting to do this. But before we go any further, I need you to be sure."

"I…" She struggled to get command of her thoughts. "I want this, too. But I'm terrified of the fallout. I'm afraid that…" Camilla looked around the interior of the car, trying to find the words.

"You're afraid I'll hurt you." Jordan collapsed against the leather seat, still holding her hand in his own. She was surprised to realize that he hadn't let go of it this entire time.

"I'm afraid that I'll let *myself* get hurt." She slowly traced the calluses he must've earned from all those years of tightly holding on to the ropes and reins, a visual reminder of the way he maintained control at all costs. "And, as shallow as this sounds, I'm afraid that other people will find out and think less of me."

"I don't know how anyone could possibly think that."

"That's because nobody has ever doubted you, Jordan. You come from a world where you're the golden prince and nobody has ever called into question what you do or how you go about doing it. You could have your pick of any woman, yet here you are with me. People are going to want to know why and eventually they'll start specu- lating that I'm using you."

"God, woman, I *wish* you would use me. I've practically been at your beck and call, at your complete disposal, these past weeks. I've served pancakes and collected trash and washed cars and read to senior citizens and somehow ended up coaching an eight-year-old girls' basketball team in the hopes that you *would* use me."

She knew that he meant the words to be light- hearted, but this was a decision she didn't want to take lightly. Camilla said as much, then added,

"If we decide to get more physical, I don't want anyone knowing."

He glanced in his rearview mirror at a cluster of people walking along the sidewalk. People were getting off work right about now and anyone who passed by might see them walk up to her apartment together.

"In that case, give me until tomorrow to plan something a little more discreet. I promise I'll make it worth the wait. And nobody will have to know." He smiled with an amount of confidence only he could exude when faced with a seemingly impossible task.

Yet nothing ever seemed impossible for Jordan.

As Camilla watched him drive away, she got a sinking feeling that she was just as much a goner as he'd claimed to be.

Chapter Nine

Jordan wanted his first time with Camilla to be perfect. And in order to do that, he needed to find somewhere away from Bronco. Someplace that was neutral territory and where his name wouldn't be recognized. One of his buddies from college had a family cabin near Great Falls that overlooked the Missouri River and, as soon as Mac left the office, Jordan made a few calls.

"It's not much to look at," Jordan warned Camilla on Tuesday morning when she asked him what she should pack. "But it's away from here and pretty isolated."

As they drove to the cabin that afternoon,

both silence and anticipation crackled in the air between them. He'd created a playlist of several songs in the hopes that if things got awkward on the long drive, they could at least listen to the same music that they'd danced to at the Denim and Diamonds event. Jordan tried not speed up the mountain roads, like an impatient youth with only one thing on his mind. Yet the closer they got to their destination, the more his nerves hummed along to the beat and the heavier his foot got on the gas pedal.

The long dirt driveway was littered with leaves, indicating no other vehicles had disturbed them recently. When he turned off the engine, Camilla climbed out of the car and studied the log structure. "It actually *is* a cabin in the woods,"

"I told you it was rustic." Jordan retrieved a box of food and Camilla's overnight bag out of the back seat. Telling himself to take his time, he decided to make a second trip for the cooler he'd packed and for his own duffel bag.

"Yeah, but I've seen your family's version of rustic." She looked at the box in his arms. "So, I'm guessing there's no private chef here?" she teased. "No concierge to fetch things for us?"

"No. But if you're lucky, I might bring you room service."

She'd shed her coat in the car and was standing before him in a blue dress printed with tiny flowers and a square neckline. It quickly occurred to him that this was the first time he'd seen her in a dress since the fundraiser gala. The thin fabric cinched at her waist before softly falling to just above her knees. It wasn't snowing again, but he was still surprised to see her long golden legs were bare except for the tan cowboy boots. Her dark hair was loose and wavy and her wide smile made his knees buckle. "What's on the menu?"

"Only one of my finest specialties," he told her, holding the box higher so she couldn't peek inside.

"That sounds fancy." She lifted up on tiptoe.

"You might want to lower your expectations, then."

She arched her brows. "All of them?"

"Well, the ones about the food. And possibly the decorations inside. Hopefully, I meet all your other expectations, though."

Camilla's cheeks flooded with color. "It's kind of weird knowing that we're here for just one reason."

"Not *just* for one reason, I hope." Jordan set the box on the front porch as he searched behind an empty flower box hanging from the windowsill. "Even if we didn't do *that*, I'd still be happy just having you out here and all to myself."

He found the hidden key and unlocked the front door, sweeping one arm forward for her to go first. As she passed by him to enter the cabin, she looked back over her shoulder and asked, "Then you're perfectly fine sitting on opposite ends of the sofa, not touching, just talking?"

He groaned as he followed her inside. "It'll be tough to manage, but I can do it."

Luckily, the brown leather love seat facing the fireplace was just as small as the one in her apartment, which meant they couldn't sit *too* far from each other. He set her bag on a round pine table and went back to the porch to retrieve the box of food. When he returned, she wasn't where he'd left her, but the sliding glass door leading out to the deck was open. He put the food in the kitchen before heading out to the car to get the cooler and his own bag.

The stuffy, stale scent of the unused cabin was soon replaced with the brisk, fir-scented air making its way inside, and he took a steadying breath. *Take it slow*, Jordan reminded himself as he walked out to the deck to join Camilla, only to find that she wasn't there.

Huh. That meant there was only one place she could be.

Heading to the master bedroom with measured steps, Jordan's heart nearly stopped when he saw her standing in front of the massive windows framing the entire wall.

"This is breathtaking." She faced him with that amazing smile and her arms spread wide open. "Who knew some rustic little cabin in the woods would have the best view in the entire state of Montana?"

Jordan barely noticed the expansive curve of the flowing river on display outside the windows behind her. "You mean the *second* best view."

He walked toward her, but he didn't have to go far. She met him halfway across the room.

Camilla's nerve endings sizzled in awareness with every taste of him. Jordan's hands splayed against her back as he held her in place to explore her mouth, the hunger in his kisses matching her own.

There was something about Jordan Taylor that made Camilla feel as though she would never have anything to worry about. He would always take care of everything. And nothing proved that more than the way his capable fingers slowly worked their way down the small buttons along the back of her dress. His knuckles softly grazed her heated skin underneath, giving the briefest taste of what was to come. Jordan always held himself back in the most subtle way, which only served to arouse her into a state of delicious anticipation.

She tried to return the favor of unbuttoning his shirt, but her fingers trembled with excitement. She pushed the crisp, starched fabric off his shoulders, allowing her palms to finally make contact with the smooth, warm wall of his wide chest.

His mouth trailed light kisses along her jaw, down to her neck. She tilted her head back, not only to allow him more access, but also so that she could gasp for more air. The silky fabric of her dress tickled her tingling skin as he eased it down her body until it landed in a pile at her feet.

"I'll be right back," Jordan whispered before disappearing from the bedroom. Camilla quickly used the opportunity to yank off her boots, and was standing in front of the bed in only her bra and panties when he returned carrying a small leather toiletries bag. He grabbed one of her hands, and she eagerly followed him over to the side table, where he put down his bag before sitting on the fluffy white comforter.

Jordan shirtless was quite a sight to behold. He was six feet of lean, athletic muscles from his broad shoulders to his chiseled biceps to his narrow waist. He pulled her closer to stand between his legs, his jaw clenched tightly as she traced her hands along the sculpted planes of his torso. When she was touching him like this, looking at him like this, every rational thought went right out the window.

Which was probably why she didn't realize her bra was gone until she felt a cool breeze on her nipple right before his skilled tongue set it on fire. Her legs threatened to give out as his mouth began a tender assault on first one breast and then the other.

A whimpering sound tickled her throat, and his steadying hands encircled her waist, holding her upright. She slowly lifted each knee to the mattress until she was straddling him. His palms moved to her rear end, cupping each cheek as he easily lifted her, keeping his mouth on her breasts as he stood and switched their positions.

Now it was her turn to rain kisses down his torso as he stood in front of her.

He remained absolutely still, his only movement the slight shuddering of his muscles as her lips memorized first his toned pecs and then the ridges of his tight abdomen. When she got to his waistband, his breath was coming hard and fast, his chest rising and falling with the frantic pounding of his heart.

Camilla nearly smiled at the thrill of finally succeeding in completely unnerving Jordan Taylor. This time, her fingers didn't tremble as she confidently unbuckled his belt and then his fly.

Her earlier fluttering of anticipation was now replaced by the boldness of determination. She wanted this man and she wanted him now.

His pants were barely down his hips when he reached for his toiletries case and pulled out a packet. Camilla took the condom from him and slid it over the length of his arousal, his groan further empowering her.

Jordan's thumbs grazed along her jawline, tilting her face up to look into his. His voice was husky and low when he said, "I wanted to make our first time absolutely perfect for you, but I don't think I can wait much longer."

"It's already perfect." Maintaining eye contact, she shifted herself toward the center of the bed and smiled at him in encouragement. "Please don't hold back on my account."

Unlike every other article of her clothing he'd removed so far, there was nothing slow or methodical in the way he desperately dragged her panties over her hips and down her legs. It was rushed, and the realization that she'd made him lose control sent another thrill spiraling through her.

He settled himself between her knees and entered her swiftly, the air rushing out of her lungs as he filled her completely. Holding himself poised above her, Jordan kissed her tenderly as she adjusted to his size. Within moments, though, Camilla rocked her hips against his as her body searched for more contact, more friction, more pressure to satisfy the throbbing desire pulsing from the deepest recesses of her core. He responded at first with short strokes that soon gave way to longer thrusts as he built a steady rhythm that had Camilla writhing with need underneath him.

His warm breath fanned her cheek as his breathing became more labored, more intense every time his hips drew away from her. She gave no thought to her own intake of air, panting desperately as she arched against him. When she brought her knees up on either side of him, Jordan sank deeper inside, and all of the coiled tension from that very first kiss on that very first night suddenly unraveled into a spiral of contractions that reverberated throughout her body until she was shuddering underneath him.

Jordan called out her name before stiffening with his own release while Camilla kept her legs wrapped around him, anchoring herself to him as they both floated into the receding waves of the most electrifying storm she'd ever experienced.

"You weren't lying about your sandwich making skills," Camilla told Jordan as he set a plate in front of her. The dual-sided fireplace was open to both the kitchen and the bedroom, but they chose to spread out a picnic on the bed so they could watch the sunset through the massive windows. "They're almost as good as your bartending skills."

"I've barely even begun showing you all my skills." He deftly pulled the cork out of a bottle of red wine.

Not waiting for him to hand her a glass, she took a bite of the most unbelievable and gravity-defying creation. Crusty, mini loaves of sourdough were stacked high with slow-roasted Taylor Beef (of course), gourmet cheese, grilled red peppers, romaine lettuce and homemade horseradish mayo. Starving, she took a second bite and swallowed before asking, "Where did you learn how to make this?"

"One summer, we had this ranch hand who had a major crush on my nanny, Rosalie. He would always ask her to go riding with him in the afternoons, but my dad used to work late and she would tell him that she couldn't go anywhere without us. He told her to bring us along, but she always found some reason why she couldn't. One day, he asks and she tells him that the chef went home early and she has to make us dinner. He goes, 'No problem. I'll make us all a picnic.' This guy proceeds to get out every possible ingredient he can find in our fridge. Brandon and I were chomping at the bit because we could care less about a picnic, we just wanted to go ride the horses. But the ranch hand took his sweet time and made these sandwiches that Rosalie couldn't stop raving about."

"They must've been pretty delicious to leave such a lasting impression on you." Camilla took a sip of the wine, which paired perfectly with the roast beef.

"Oh, I couldn't even tell you what they tasted like. I was ten and remembered thinking that it would've been just as good and a heck of a lot quicker if he'd slapped some peanut butter and grape jelly on a couple of slices of bread. But every night that week, we got to go out for an evening ride because that man knew how to make a damn good sandwich. It suddenly seemed like an important life skill I needed to master. So I did."

Camilla laughed. "So what happened to Rosalie and this ranch hand? Did they live happily ever after?"

"No. It turns out that the ranch hand was also making sandwiches for the woman who cleaned the bunkhouse on Saturdays. And the cocktail waitress over at Wild Wesley's in town. And possibly Daphne's ballet teacher, but that was never confirmed."

"Oh, my gosh, Jordan." Camilla giggled then threw a pillow at him. "We're sharing this wonderful romantic dinner and that has to be about the least romantic story you could possibly tell me."

"What?" Jordan shrugged, then grinned. "It's not like *I'm* out making sandwiches for anyone else."

Camilla's face went warm and her stomach no longer felt empty. In fact, every part of her body felt blissfully full. Almost complete. "Are you saying that you're not dating anyone else but me?"

He drank his wine, while his eyes drank her in. Then he took her plate from her and set it on the nightstand. "Even if I had the time, which I don't because I'm always busy chasing you, why would I want to when I've got everything I need right here?"

Instead of debating the answer, she let him pull her back down to the sheets and within seconds she had completely forgotten about sandwiches and everything else.

Camilla took one last look at the log structure and already felt a yearning pull at her belly before they'd even left the driveway the following morning. She was going to miss everything about this perfect cabin in the woods, from the gorgeous views of the river beyond the bedroom windows to the equally gorgeous view of a very naked Jordan standing at the tiny kitchen counter as he made her a midnight snack.

She would miss the single stall shower where Jordan crowded in next to her, lathering her back with soap as he sang a Beyoncé song, just as much as she would miss the spacious rag rug in front of the fireplace where the only singing came from Camilla's cries of ecstasy as he lathered her front with his tongue.

She would miss the outside balcony—which was larger than the combined living and dining rooms—where they braved the cold for their morning coffee, just as much as she would miss the cozy cocoon of the bedcovers where they braved the intense warmth of their shared body heat just so they could sleep in each other's arms.

This idyllic cabin represented everything they could have if only their own lives back home weren't so different. Yet as Jordan steered the car toward the main road, the realities of life threatened to pop that perfect bubble they'd created for themselves out here so far away from everyone else.

In fact, that bubble popped much sooner than Camilla expected when his cellular service returned and his phone lit up and buzzed like a restaurant pager notifying a customer that his table was ready.

"Sorry," he said, glancing at the dashboard screen indicating a call coming through. "I really should take this."

At least he waited until Camilla gave him an approving nod before he tapped the phone icon and answered. "What's going on, Mac?"

"Sorry to bug you with this, sport, but we've got an issue with the Oakmont account." His assistant immediately started describing what sounded like a suspended delivery due to an unpaid invoice and Camilla tried to catch the details, but the entire time all she could think about was the fact that this was a first.

In all the times they'd spent together or near each other—even on weekdays—Jordan had never taken a work call. Sure, there was that one date when they flew in the helicopter and he had the meeting with his distributor, but when he was *with* her, he was always present. Up until now, Camilla had, for the most part, been his sole focus. Of course she had never expected him to devote all of his attention to her all of the time. He had other responsibilities and a business to run. It was just that she hadn't expected him to shift gears and return to business mode so quickly.

"I'll take care of it, Mac," Jordan said. "Can you connect me to my dad's office?"

As he waited on hold for his assistant to transfer him, Camilla felt a shiver travel down her neck. Did Mac know they'd spent the night together? She seemed to know everything else about her boss.

Would his father find out?

Did it matter if he did? She tried to scold herself for caring about it one way or the other, but all the twists and turns down the mountain road threatened her rational thoughts.

Originally, she had wanted to keep their relationship a secret. But her family knew about it, as did Daphne. Cornelius had even seen them riding together, so he must at least suspect something was going on. However, there was a big difference between casually dating and spending the night together.

The call was dropped several times because of the spotty reception and when Jordan finally got through to his father's assistant, he cursed because the man told him that Cornelius was out of the office. But of course the very determined Jordan wasn't going to simply let it go at that. She knew firsthand that he'd go after what he wanted until he got it.

Jordan disconnected and, without explanation or apology, pulled up the contact number for his father, which weirdly was listed on his phone as Cornelius Taylor III rather than the informal Dad. When Cornelius answered, his booming voice echoed on speaker in the confines of the car.

"This had better be important, Jordan," his

father said by way of greeting. "I'm about to walk into that press luncheon with the governor."

"Dad, please tell me you didn't stop delivery to Oakmont on the day before Thanksgiving." Something about the commanding tone of Jordan's voice made Camilla pause in her own thoughts of what she planned to say to him when he finished his business call. Maybe this was more serious than a past due account.

"They're over fourteen months behind on their payments, Jordan. Taylor Beef isn't a charity operation."

"I gave them a grace period." Jordan picked up Camilla's hand and softly kissed each finger almost absentmindedly as he began speaking to his father about trade agreements and financial solvency and fluctuating market prices.

Cornelius Taylor gave no indication that he knew someone else was in the car with his son, and Camilla would've felt guilty for listening in on the call if she wasn't becoming slightly aroused by both his touch and his impressive business knowledge.

Cornelius countered with arguments about other customers and disproportionate pricing and enforcing legal contracts. Halfway through his father's explanation, Jordan rolled his eyes and mouthed the word *sorry* to Camilla.

"I'm gonna stop you there, Dad," he finally

interrupted. A tingle raced up her arm and it wasn't just from the skilled way his thumb was now stroking her knuckles as he used his other hand to deftly steer the sports car along the winding road down the mountain. Jordan's response to his father was informed and well-articulated as he cited last quarter's profit and loss margins and rattled off the stock market's most recent closing numbers for shares of the biggest beef companies from the United States to Japan to Brazil.

This wasn't some rich kid working for the family business, she realized, as he continued to astonish her with his knowledge and insight. Jordan wasn't having this conversation, though, to impress her. He was simply being himself and, in doing so, providing her with a glimpse of his daily life.

"At the end of the day," Jordan finished, "the amount they owe us is a drop in the bucket and barely affects our bottom line."

"But it's the principle, son. You give somebody something for free and they'll just keep coming back and taking advantage of you. There's no place for emotion in business."

"Dad, Oakmont is a homeless shelter and this is their busiest time of the year," Jordan replied, and Camilla suddenly understood why he'd been so focused on responding to this particular problem. "It also falls under my scope as the VP of Operations for the company. You need to let me handle it."

"Fine. But between your bleeding heart and Daphne's, don't be surprised if our family ends up in the poorhouse."

"According to our estate attorneys and an ironclad trust fund, I don't have to worry about those types of surprises. Besides, Dad, your heart could do with a little bleeding."

"Nope. The last charity case who got too close to my heart nearly bled me dry," Cornelius said, then disconnected without so much as a goodbye.

"Give me one more minute," Jordan said to Camilla as he turned onto the county highway that would take them to Bronco. "I need to make two more calls."

First he called Mac and gave her instructions for reinstating the Oakmont account. Next, he called the director of Oakmont and personally apologized for the misunderstanding. "We'll have a delivery truck out to you this afternoon."

By the time he got off the phone, they were almost to Camilla's apartment, and she understood why they called him the Smoother.

When he parked his car in the alley below her front porch in the spot she was starting to think of as his, Camilla turned to him and asked,

"Was your dad referring to the Denim and Diamonds gala?"

"When?" Jordan asked.

"When he said that the last charity case nearly bled him dry. I assumed he was talking about the fundraiser he hosted."

"Oh, no. My dad thinks it's a clever play of words to refer to his ex-wives as charity cases. And to him, any time his net worth dips below nine figures, he thinks he's practically going bankrupt."

Her eyes widened at the revelation of the Taylors' financial standing before she blinked back her own insecurities. Would everyone else in his family think of *her* as one of Jordan's charity cases? She gulped and murmured, "How charming."

"Actually, if he'd known you were listening, he would've laid the charm on real thick, like he does for everyone else. But the real Cornelius Taylor isn't the best businessman. He's been burned by a few business associates that he thought were friends, and he's been targeted by scores of gold diggers in his lifetime. He always thinks everyone is out to take advantage of him."

And of his son, Camilla thought. But she didn't want to say that aloud and cast any shadows on their perfect night together.

Chapter Ten

"Jordan, where is your family today?" Dante asked as they gathered around the Sanchezes's dining table on Thursday afternoon.

"My dad and stepmom are hosting my uncles and a few of their friends at their house for Thanksgiving," he answered as he passed the bowl of stuffing to Dylan. "They invited us, but when Camilla told me how important the holiday is to your family, I didn't want her to miss all these traditional dishes."

Camilla wrinkled her nose at the lime-green gelatin-and-fruit salad molded in the shape of a ring before she shot him a questioning look. "They invited *me*?"

Well, not specifically. Cornelius had asked if he planned on bringing a "plus one" and then blew a gasket when Jordan said he wouldn't be home at all for the Thanksgiving meal. But the plus one would've been Camilla, so that counted as an invite, right?

Jordan shrugged. "I didn't bring it up before because I figured we'd be a lot more comfortable here."

Dylan pointed an accusatory turkey leg at him. "Doesn't your family like Camilla?"

"They've only met her once." Jordan twisted the cloth napkin in his lap as all the eyes at the table turned toward him. "My family can be a bit overwhelming. At least, some of them can."

"I bet your family's food is way better than Mrs. Waters's grandmother's runny creamed onions, though," Sophia said, refusing to take a spoonful of the untouched dish before shoving it at Felix, who also refused to accept it.

Jordan knew better than to answer that. He also knew better than to laugh too much at the Sanchez siblings' ongoing teasing and complaining about the so-called traditional Thanksgiving dishes, especially since this was their family's way of commemorating their first holiday in America. Yet even *he* couldn't argue with the fact that this was actually one of the least appetizing meals he'd ever experienced at their house.

On the other hand, it was also one of the most fun meals because they were now including him in their family's inside jokes. In fact, the more often he visited the Sanchezes, the more at home he felt here, as though they were truly starting to accept him.

Plus, the food wasn't really all that bad, especially not after Mr. Sanchez brought out a couple of bottles of chilled sauvignon blanc to help wash everything down. Jordan helped himself to one of the tastier items on the table and stared at it for a few seconds before asking, "So the rolls just come from the can like this?"

"Wait. You mean your fancy chef doesn't make crescent rolls up at the ranch?" Sophia giggled before realizing nobody else was joining in. In fact, the normally rambunctious table had grown extremely quiet.

"What?" Sophia held up a butter knife. "Are we all going to keep on pretending we don't know who he is?"

"Who is he?" Dante whispered across the table to Dylan, who shook his head in confusion.

Camilla squeezed Jordan's knee under the table, and he wasn't sure if it was meant as a reassuring gesture or a warning to remain quiet. She darted a glance at her sister. "You knew?"

"Obviously. I loaned you the dress to go to his party, remember? Besides, I work in a boutique in Bronco Heights. Half of my customers are socialites actively talking about him and his reputation."

Jordan gulped down his wine so quickly, he nearly choked.

Camilla pressed her lips together before shooting a nervous look toward their mother.

"You both might as well own up to it." Mrs. Sanchez dumped more salt onto some boiled butternut squash. "Mrs. Waters called him out in the salon in front of everyone."

Camilla cocked her head at him. "Why didn't you tell me my mom knew?"

Jordan pointed at his mouth, which was full of the mashed potatoes he'd purposely stuffed in there to prevent him from having to answer anything.

"Is there even anyone else to tell?" Camilla asked, scanning the people around the table.

"How could I *not* know?" Mr. Sanchez sat back in his seat at the head of the table and used a napkin to wipe his mouth. "I've been a mail carrier for the past thirty years and there's only three Jordans in this town."

"Here he goes with the mail-carrier-knows-everything bit." Sofia rolled her eyes. "Settle in, everyone."

Mr. Sanchez gave his youngest child a dismissive glance before continuing. "Like I was saying, one is a nine-year-old boy who writes a postcard to Santa Claus every year asking for a puppy. He's up to five dogs now and, according to his latest postcard in the North Pole drop box, he's asking for a sixth. Speaking of which, I need to give his parents the heads-up."

"You could've given *me* the heads-up that you already knew," Camilla muttered under her breath.

"Is this story going somewhere, Dad?" Dylan drummed his fingers on either side of his plate.

Mr. Sanchez took another sip of wine, apparently not the least bothered that everyone else at the table was now sitting on the edges of their seats as he took his time with his long-winded explanation. "The second one is the Montgomerys' daughter, who is away at Montana State right now. Her name is spelled J-O-R-D-Y-N-N, though, so I guess that doesn't count."

"Dad," Dylan interrupted. "*None* of this counts unless you tell us who the other Jordan in town is."

"Then there's the Jordan whose legal physical address is technically 408 Old Bronco Highway. However, he receives all his personal mail at the Taylor Beef headquarters." Mr. Sanchez's words hung in the air as the remaining family members pieced it together.

Jordan, though, wasn't about to be ashamed

of who he was. He sat up straighter and draped one arm across the back of Camilla's chair. This time when she put her hand on his thigh, it was not only reassuring, it was almost possessive. As though she was also claiming him in front of her family. His chest filled with pride, even as he squared himself for the onslaught of opinions that would surely follow. After all, the Sanchez family usually had plenty of opinions.

"Daaang," Dante said slowly as his brow creased into a V above his nose. "You're *that* Jordan Taylor? And nobody thought it was something to share with me and Dylan and Felix?"

Felix didn't seem upset, though. In fact, he'd found a sudden interest in the cranberry sauce that had been completely ignored until now.

"Hold up." The legs of Dylan's chair screeched against the hardwood floor as he shoved himself away from the table to jump up. He pointed an accusing finger at his oldest brother. "Felix *did* know! That's why he chose Jordan for basketball the very first night. You went to high school with him and knew he held all those athletic records. You've been keeping Jordan to yourself all this time."

At that, the entire table erupted and instead of anyone berating Jordan for keeping a secret— not that he'd technically kept it a secret—they all accused each other of knowing exactly who he was, but never discussing it.

Voices were raised and overlapped other voices, and the only thing he could make out was that everyone kept their knowledge to themselves because they were afraid of how the others would react if they'd known he was one of *those* Taylors. Except for Felix, who kept the knowledge to himself so he could keep beating his brothers on the basketball court.

Since none of the arguing was currently directed his way, Jordan used the ongoing distraction as an excuse to pull his vibrating cell phone from his back pocket. It had gone off several times during the meal, but he hadn't wanted to be rude and answer it at the table. When he saw the text from his father, though, he nearly groaned.

"What is it?" Camilla whispered and leaned toward him. He showed her the display screen.

You need to get here and deal with your sister.

"You should probably go," Camilla said. Was she saying that because she wanted him gone? Because now that her family knew who he was, she was suddenly embarrassed of him? Or maybe she wanted to protect him from the fallout—when all the Sanchezes stopped arguing among each other and decided to team up to demand that she stop dating him. Because despite their teasing and trash talk, Jordan knew without a doubt that this family would band together to protect one of their own.

Not that Camilla needed to be protected from him.

Regardless of what was transpiring with Camilla and her family, though, Jordan couldn't stay here and leave Daphne hanging.

"You're right. I really should go." He let out the breath he hadn't realized he'd been holding. "Any chance I could talk you into coming with me?"

"It sounds like a private family matter. I'm sure your father wouldn't want me there."

And just like that, the arguing at the table stopped suddenly and everyone shifted curious eyes to Camilla and Jordan.

"I've got a text from my father." Jordan held up his phone. "Something has come up and I need to go home."

"Oh, did Daddy summon you back to the ranch for pumpkin pie?" Dylan asked, but the normal teasing didn't seem so playful now that they knew who his father was.

Or maybe this rush of defensiveness pressing against Jordan's chest was due to the fact that he had, technically, just been summoned.

Either way, now wasn't the time for Jordan to show weakness or shame. All of the Sanchezes appreciated people standing up for themselves and if he truly wanted to fit in with them, he needed to give as good as he got.

So he looked Camilla's brother in the eye and said, "Don't worry, Dylan. I'll give you time to digest all that turkey and then I'll come back to demonstrate that box out reversal move on the basketball court."

Dylan snorted, but had a smile on his face. "Oh, I don't need a demonstration. In fact, I plan to show *you* a thing or two."

Someone suggested that it might snow tonight, making the court slippery. This caused another eruption of smack talk between all the brothers with Mr. Sanchez playing referee. Once again, Jordan used the distraction to talk privately with Camilla. To hopefully convince her that it would actually be more beneficial to have her with him.

"Daphne knows you, so taking you there with me will make her feel like she has more support," he told her. "Plus, my father typically causes less of a scene when there are witnesses around. I told you how he is about appearances and all that."

What he didn't tell her was that she would likely be jumping feetfirst into the Taylor family drama. His dad and sister loved each other, but they'd been butting heads for a long time now, the buildup of tension only making their battle lines more rigid. The showdown would likely be an emotional tug-of-war.

If Camilla could survive that, then he was certain she would finally realize that there was nothing else keeping them from being together.

Camilla's stomach did somersaults as they drove up the main driveway of the Taylor Ranch. While it felt good that Jordan wanted her by his side, she was certain that nobody else in the Taylor family would be happy to see her.

The first sign that something was wrong was when they pulled up to the main house and Daphne's vehicle wasn't in sight.

"She must've already left," Jordan said as he put his car in Park.

He took Camilla's hand as they walked toward the ten-feet-high custom-made oak front doors. From far away, the house had been impressive. Yet standing on the sprawling log-beamed porch, which was easily bigger than the entire cabin they'd shared in Great Falls, was downright overwhelming.

The massive entryway they passed through was larger than most hotel lobbies and way better decorated. She barely had time to take in the tasteful and obviously expensive furnishings as Jordan pulled her behind him toward a dining room with a table long enough to seat at least thirty people.

Judging by the abandoned silver place settings, china plates and crystal goblets, there had likely been at least that many people here earlier. But now only Cornelius sat at the head of the table, his pretty young wife to the right of him.

"Look who finally shows up," the silver-haired patriarch barked. Holding court in his throne-sized chair, Cornelius Taylor seemed as though he relished his role of monarch of his own royal kingdom.

"What's going on?" Jordan asked, his jaw tighter than Camilla had ever seen it.

"What's going on is that Jessica spent several weeks planning this dinner and it was totally ruined."

Jordan's fingers were rigid against hers, but he kept her hand in his. "How was it ruined?"

"The table was set with place cards and everything. Your uncles and cousins and all of our most important neighbors and friends were here. But when it was time for Gallagher to serve the meal, those two seats at the end—" Cornelius pointed to the opposite end of the table "—were still empty."

"I really didn't mind having empty seats." Jessica tentatively patted the older man's hand as it gripped the ornate wood of his armrest. Camilla wanted to tell poor Jessica that her husband clearly wasn't offended on *her* behalf. He was annoyed that his plans had been thwarted. That he hadn't gotten what he wanted.

"I apologize for the misunderstanding, Jessica." Jordan bowed his head toward his young stepmother. "But I told my father last night that we were having Thanksgiving dinner with Camilla's family."

Cornelius's frown got even deeper, if that was possible. "And *I* told her that you would come to your senses and stop chasing tail long enough to do your family duty."

Camilla gasped, tasting a bitterness in her throat. She'd been mentally prepared for the old man to suggest that she was after Jordan for his money. But she hadn't quite expected him to insinuate that Jordan was only using her for sex.

Before she could defend herself, Jordan had shifted himself in front of her. His intent might've been to block her from his father's attacks, but now all she could focus on was the tension stretching across his shoulders. His voice was cold and rock-steady when he said, "I've already told you that Camilla is much more than that, so I suggest you watch what you say."

Okay, so maybe some of the bitterness building inside her was eased when she heard Jordan readily jump to her defense. His warning to his father definitely gave her a boost of courage to step around his blocking back, resuming her place by his side. Just in time to see Cornelius roll his eyes to the monstrous crystal chandelier above.

"My apologies, miss." Cornelius gazed down his nose at Camilla, his tone sounding anything but apologetic. "I'm sure you're not just another one of my son's passing fancies, and I have no place pointing out to him how much he stands to lose by getting involved with the wrong girl."

"Just stop with the passive aggressive comments, Dad." Jordan shoved a hand through his hair. "You always go for the hidden insult when you know you can't win. This is why we didn't come tonight. I didn't want to subject Camilla to your whole dog and pony show. It's your own fault that you still set a place for us at the table after I clearly told you we wouldn't be attending."

She tapped Jordan on the back and pointed to the names written on the two place cards disposed of on the side table. Jordan Taylor and Daphne Taylor. "I don't think anyone was actually expecting me to show up."

Instead of relishing the fact that she'd been right all along, that she would never be welcomed in Jordan's world, Camilla's heart was trying not to sag like the used linen napkins carelessly discarded along the once carefully laid table.

"Do you know what it's like to have my own two children, my very own flesh and blood, turn their backs on me?" Cornelius continued on unfazed, underscoring the fact that Camilla's personal feelings—even her presence—were secondary to the real reason he'd summoned Jordan out to the ranch like a naughty child. "And on Thanksgiving, of all times, when everyone is here to witness it firsthand?"

"Where's Daph, Dad?" Jordan's biceps was a coil of tense muscle, his hand clenched beside hers. "Your text made it sound as though I needed to come out here immediately to talk with her. You made it sound like something was wrong."

"It is!" Cornelius slammed a fist on the table, rattling the crystal water goblet near him. "She refused to come to dinner unless Jessica added alternative dishes to the menu. What was that damn concoction she mentioned? Plant-based turkey? As if we'd ever serve anything so ridiculous under this roof."

"It really was no problem," Jessica murmured, patting her husband's hand again. "I could've had the chef prepare—"

"No." Cornelius put his palm up, dismissing his wife in midsentence. "This vegetarian phase of hers has gone on long enough. First she makes a mockery out of me—out of our family legacy—by running that Hippie Hearts animal shelter, whatever the hell that is. Then she wants to sit at my table, in front of all my friends, like some sort of social justice warrior lording her meatless righteousness over us. She's turning me into a complete laughingstock."

"Dad, you're really overreacting. Daphne's dietary decisions have nothing to do with you."

"We make our living by turning cattle into steaks and she wants to make her living by saving them. It goes against everything we stand for. Taylor Beef money was good enough for her growing up, but now she wants to publicly turn up her nose at us. When are you going to wake up, son? This is what women do. They take and take until they can't use you anymore." His scathing words even made his young wife's mouth drop open. "Even your sister—"

"I'm going to cut you off right there, Mr. Taylor," Camilla interrupted. The anger roiling through her had propelled her forward to stand in front of Jordan. "I don't know what kind of people you've surrounded yourself with before now, but that is *not* what women do. And if your neighbors and so-called friends allow you to talk about other women this way, then they are not your true friends. They're your minions. I've heard you make several disparaging comments about charity cases and chasing tail, and someone needs to tell you once and for all that blaming women for your unhappiness reflects more poorly on *you* and your decisions than it does on the women in your life. In fact, thinking everyone is only interested in your money doesn't make you sound powerful. It makes you sound scared."

Cornelius's face had gone a blustery shade of red and his eyes narrowed into angry slits. Yet he kept his voice measured as he said, "Thank you, Carol, for your insight into something that is absolutely none of your business. This is a family matter and you would do well to take yourself back to the Valley."

"If you know that I'm from the Valley, sir, then you also know damn well that my name is Camilla. So let's not play this game where you pretend that you haven't had a team of paid informants looking into my background the second you found out that Jordan and I were in a relationship."

"We've moved on from dating to a relationship now?" Jordan whispered out the side of his mouth. Camilla whipped her head in his direction and he twisted his lower lip. "Never mind. Keep going."

"Well, whatever you guys want to call it," Cornelius said as he wagged a finger between them. "This thing between you two won't last."

"Now, Cornelius..." Jessica tutted quietly. It wasn't really a reprimand, but her attempt to at least redirect her husband, to nearly stand up to him, energized Camilla. Even if she ruined things between Jordan and his father, at least she might have empowered another woman.

"Maybe it *will* last." Camilla let the threat hang in the air for a few seconds. "And maybe it won't. But either way, the future of our relationship won't be something you can control. Contrary to whatever bull you've been feeding yourself, Mr. Taylor, your children have their own minds and their own personalities and their own journeys. Jordan is no more like you than Daphne is, and he's a better man for it."

As soon as Camilla said the words aloud, she realized that she really believed it. Jordan was nothing like this bitter, high-handed braggart.

Cornelius stood up and tossed his napkin on the table. "I'm not going to sit in my own house and listen to some waitress tell me how I should run my family."

Camilla, though, couldn't let him storm out of the dining room without one last parting shot.

"Well, even this waitress knows that you can run a business, but you can't run a family. As soon as you make peace with that, you'll be a happier man."

Her heart was thudding in her chest when Jordan slipped his hand from hers. Had she been out of line? Had she gone too far? Instead of following his father, though, he wrapped his arm around her waist and led her to the door. "Let's get out of here."

Exactly three weeks after first feeling like a gatecrasher at one of their fancy parties, Camilla was actually being escorted off the Taylor Ranch.

Possibly for good this time.

Chapter Eleven

"I'm sorry." Camilla finally broke the tense silence when Jordan turned onto Old Bronco Highway. "I really overstepped. I never should have—"

"Are you kidding?" Jordan cut in. "You were magnificent. Hardly anyone ever stands up to my old man like that and I've never been more impressed. So please don't be sorry for telling him what very few people have the guts to say."

"Oh, I wasn't apologizing for what I said to him." The edges of Camilla's tongue were still tingling with defensiveness, though she'd lost some of her earlier sizzle. "I was expressing my condolences that you have to deal with that guy on a regular basis."

Jordan made a scratchy chuckle at first before bursting out in a full laugh. Like a cork being popped out of a champagne bottle, Camilla felt some of her own tension fizzle with his release.

He caught his breath long enough to ask, "Did you see his face when you told him he looked weak and pitiful?"

"Oh, my gosh." Camilla giggled, feeling all that earlier pressure lifting from her shoulders. "I turned to Jessica to see if she was going to start fanning him with her napkin because he looked like he was going to blow a gasket."

He erupted into another fit of laughter, which was so contagious, she couldn't help but join in. Even though it felt wrong to be laughing at his father's expense, relief washed through her, knowing that Jordan wasn't angry with her.

"But seriously," he said on a sobering breath. "Remember when I told you that I see things differently when I'm with you? I've gotten so immune to my father's blustering and his control tactics over the years that I was oblivious to how everyone else saw him. I can brush him off when he insults me, but I hated the way he spoke to you. He was completely out of line and you didn't deserve his condescension."

Thankfully, Jordan didn't make any excuses for his father, nor did he downplay the man's pointed comments. Maybe he really was starting to understand what she would have to put up with if they ended up together.

Camilla sighed as she leaned back in the leather seat, watching the flickering colors whizzing by her window. The Thanksgiving dinner leftovers were barely put away, yet people were already stringing up their Christmas lights. She never understood how folks could so easily move on from one thing to the next.

It brought to mind Cornelius Taylor's comment about Jordan chasing tail. Deep down, she knew that the older man's goal wasn't really to insult her. His goal was to get his son back under his thumb. She was just collateral damage.

But it didn't make the insult hurt any less.

When they stopped at an intersection, Jordan lifted his hand and gently stroked her cheek with the back of his fingers until she turned to look at him. "I am really sorry for putting you through that. I'm especially sorry for dragging you away from your own family's house and ruining your holiday."

"You didn't ruin my holiday, Jordan," she said, her eyes blinking back a sudden threat of dampness. Admitting otherwise would be like admitting that his father had the power to hurt her, which would be like admitting that, deep down, she wanted the Taylors to accept her the way the Sanchezes had clearly accepted Jordan.

So she forced a smile instead. "Although I'm pretty bummed that I missed out on the only good part of our Thanksgiving meal."

"The after-dinner basketball game?" he asked.

"No, the pumpkin pie. Mrs. Waters can't make a casserole to save her life, but her pie recipes are out of this world."

Jordan laughed, then drove her back to the Sanchez house. Thankfully, most of her siblings had already gone back to their own places and she was able to sneak out of her parents' kitchen with a prepacked bag of leftovers, half of a pecan pie—the pumpkin was long gone—and no questions about the drama at Taylor Ranch.

The adrenaline from her earlier encounter with Cornelius had drained just as quickly as it had spiked, leaving Camilla's body depleted and her mind emotionally exhausted. She didn't want to talk right that second or even eat. All she wanted was to spend the evening wrapped in the warmth of Jordan's arms. By the time they reached her apartment, it was pretty much a foregone conclusion that he would be coming upstairs with her. At least, for her it was. She knew he would never push for it unless she asked.

Following her, he carried the bag of leftovers up the stairs. The pie tin was balanced in one of her uplifted palms as she used her free hand to unlock the door. While she was distracted, Jordan shot an arm around her waist and turned her toward him. "I've been waiting all day for this, and I don't want to wait another minute."

He kissed her gently, slowly building the pressure of his lips and skillful tongue until Camilla couldn't have told him good-night even if she'd wanted to. So she did what any sane, red-blooded woman would do.

Still balancing the pie, she playfully slipped her hand down the front of his shirt until she got to his waistband. Then she grabbed the most accessible thing—his belt buckle—and pulled him inside her apartment so she could finish what he'd started.

Jordan stretched his arms over his head as he watched Camilla sleep curled up beside him in her bed. He could've stayed like this all morning, but the constant buzzing of his cell phone on the bedside table was becoming increasingly difficult to ignore.

Normally, he never bothered with the notifications from Taylor Beef's marketing team, but he couldn't disregard the three missed calls from Mac. Or her text message in all caps that said, CHECK OUT THE POST ON @AllThingsBronco.

Ugh. Mac knew Jordan hated those ridiculous social media accounts that were no better than the sleazy tabloids. He was about to set the phone down unanswered but another notification alert pinged on his phone, this time from Daphne. You better do something about this, Jor.

His chest rumbled with a groan, which made Camilla stir awake. She pressed her warm and very nude body closer to his before lifting her sleepy, sexy eyes to his face. He was more than tempted to toss the phone to the nearby sofa until she asked, "What's wrong?"

"I'm not sure. I'm guessing it's some sort of article or social media post about Daphne not showing up at my dad's last night for dinner. The people posting these things never have all the facts and always make a big deal out of nothing." He clicked on the link Daphne and Mac had both sent him.

When he saw the image fill his screen he groaned again. When he read the bold caption underneath, he cursed.

"Is it that bad?" Camilla sat up, taking the top sheet with her. "Poor Daphne."

"It's not about my sister."

She took the phone from him. He scrubbed his hands across the stubble on his jaw and then his eyes. Unfortunately, he couldn't unsee the bold caption under the picture of him and Camilla standing on her tiny porch last night, kissing.

Bronco's Most Eligible Bachelor in Torrid
Affair with Waitress

The angle of the photo meant it was likely shot
from the sidewalk across the street, where the
only nearby businesses were an antiques shop
and a dry cleaner, two places that would've been
closed on a Thanksgiving evening. "Someone
must've been following us last night."

"Perhaps. Your Tesla certainly stands out in
this neighborhood," Camilla said rather calmly.
With as much effort as she'd taken to keep their
relationship a secret, she certainly wasn't showing any emotion now that they'd been found out.
In fact, her tone was purely casual when she
pointed out, "The way I'm holding up the pecan
pie like a serving tray nicely underscores the fact
that I'm just a waitress."

He sat up in the bed. "Come on, Camilla, you
know you're so much more than that."

"Of course I know that, Jordan. But it still
doesn't seem to stop anyone from commenting
on my job title." She didn't have to point out
that his father had also made the same reference last night.

Jordan retrieved the phone from her and only
made it through the first few comments before
he felt steam practically expel from his eyeballs.

How could people be so absolutely mean about someone they'd never met? So absolutely crude?

It was one thing for him to ignore the haters when he was the target of their snide opinions and disparaging nicknames. It was quite another to see them so blatantly insulting Camilla. She'd done nothing to deserve any of this.

His fingers flew over the keyboard as he composed several scathing retorts before deleting them all. "You know what? These jerks don't deserve a response. Half of them can't even use proper grammar. I mean, what the hell is a 'goal digger'?"

Camilla lifted her eyebrows as though he should already know, which he did. Then she stood and grabbed the nearest article of clothing on her floor—his cashmere sweater—and slid it over her head. Without saying a word, she padded the twelve or so feet to the kitchen and switched on her coffee maker. "You think that's bad? Slide to the next picture in the post and see what some creative thinkers wrote there."

Jordan set his feet on the floor, but that didn't brace him for the next image. It was of Camilla—still holding that pecan pie—using her other hand to pull on his belt as she led him inside. The caption said:

Grabbing the bull by the horn, or in this case, the Rancher by the—

Jordan couldn't look away from some of the disgusting comments people were making on *that one*. But ultimately, the consensus was the same. They thought Camilla was an opportunist and not good enough for the Charmed Prince of Bronco Heights.

"How are you being so calm about this?" he asked as he yanked on his discarded pants.

"Because I expected this all along." She shrugged. "Any female who dates you must know that her name is going to get thrown to the wolves. When those females are wealthy socialites, the wolves might sniff around a bit before getting bored and moving on. But when it's someone like me—someone who shouldn't even be able to reach the social ladder, let alone climb it—then it's gonna be an open feast."

Guilt rocked through Jordan. She was right. She'd even tried to warn him, but he blew her off, thinking that it couldn't possibly be this bad. "So how do you think we should handle this?"

"There's nothing to handle." Again Camilla shrugged, and her indifference affected him more than anything else had. What had happened to the woman who'd fought for him last night? Jordan watched her in confusion as she took a sip of coffee then added, "Stuff like this is going to happen no matter what we say. And if people think we're together, it'll happen even more."

"They *better* think we're together," Jordan said louder than he intended. "They also better think that I'm not going to sit by while a bunch of strangers make insulting comments about you on social media."

Camilla hesitated and in that moment, he saw she wasn't completely indifferent. "I'm not sure that's such a good idea."

"Look." He reached up to trace the outline of her face and ended by sliding his fingers into her silky hair as he cupped her head. She leaned into him somewhat reluctantly. "Last night, you admitted that we were in a relationship. I know we agreed on three weeks, six official dates, before we made any final decisions. Now that we've come this far, though, there's no way either one of us is willing to throw all of that away."

"Be very careful about what you're committing to, Jordan." Her eyes searched his. "If we continue to see each other, this will be our reality. If we're going to come out and tell everyone that we're a couple, we will have to deal with the backlash."

He planted his feet apart and pulled her closer to him. "I'm up for the challenge."

Her chuckle was forced, but he wasn't kidding. This time, she drew her hands up to his jaw and cupped his face. "Come on, Jordan. Let's not kid ourselves. You've walked away from a number of relationships over a lot less than some negative publicity. The truth is, we've only known each other a few weeks. Before rushing into a full-blown relationship, maybe we should just take it slow and see how this all plays out."

"I don't want to take it slow." He stepped back and stretched his arms over his head. "Hell, Camilla, I want the whole damn world to know."

"That's easy for you to say." She braced one hand on the kitchen counter. "You're not the one they're calling a gold digger. Your business won't be affected by any of this. However, the business I'm trying to launch—the one I've been dreaming about and planning for the past six years—will depend on my reputation. I might be able to thumb my nose at these types of posts while we're together. But what happens when we break up?"

Break up? The words were a punch to his solar plexus. "You've barely admitted we're in a relationship and now you're already thinking about dumping me?"

"I'm thinking about what will happen down the road. If we break up, which is entirely possible since we barely even know each other, then I'm going to be the one who looks like the evil money grubber. The one who failed to sink her hooks into you. You'll always be the Prince Charming who made a dashing escape."

"Nobody will ever think that about you," he argued. How could anyone think Camilla Sanchez was anything less than perfect and smart and amazing?

She marched over to where he'd left his phone and tapped on the display screen. "They already do."

"Then I'll tell them that they're all wrong."

"Of course you will. Or better yet, why don't you have Cornelius Taylor issue one of his royal commands?"

After everything she'd witnessed last night between him and his old man, he was surprised by how much her words stung. "Are you comparing me to my father?"

"No. Maybe. I don't know." She rubbed her temples. "All I'm trying to say is that you can't go around telling people *how* they should feel or *what* they should believe."

He shoved his hands into his pockets and dropped his head. He'd gone from anger to desperation to shame in the blink of five minutes. The last emotion wasn't something he wanted to dwell on. He was a successful businessman who didn't back down from a challenge or a negotiation.

Jordan sucked in a deep breath through his nose, inhaling every ounce of determination he could harness. When he dragged his eyes up to

Camilla's beautiful face he said, "I'm not going to tell you how to feel. But I'm also not going to apologize to you—or to anyone else—for how *I* feel."

"Look, Jordan, it's been an intense few days and I have to go back to work tonight. Maybe it's best if we just let the dust settle a little bit before either one of us says something we might later regret."

"Fine." He snatched his shirt off the floor, not bothering to put on his boots before walking out into the cold, harsh reality of morning. He didn't even care that people might be hanging out on the street in front of her apartment, hoping for a photo of Jordan Taylor doing the walk of shame.

Frustration grew with each bare step he took. He was frustrated with the anonymous social media haters for commenting on things that were none of their business. He was frustrated with Camilla for not believing in their relationship. He was frustrated with his father because, well, because he was always frustrated with his old man and would think of the reason later.

But mostly, he was frustrated with himself and his complete lack of control over the situation.

How had it all gone wrong so fast?

That weekend, Camilla threw herself into work. And when she wasn't doing that, she threw herself into her plans for her new restaurant and putting the finishing touches on her Integrated Project for school. She'd already given her two-week notice at DJ's Deluxe and had even opened escrow on the old library building in Bronco Valley, which needed a ton of repairs.

She told herself that she was too busy to worry about Jordan and what he wanted right this second. She told herself that by not answering his calls immediately, she was giving him the chance to see that he would be fine without her. She told herself that the only way either one of them would be able to think clearly and evaluate their relationship was if there was some distance between them.

What she couldn't tell herself, though, was that not seeing him, not hearing his voice for several days, had only made her miss him more.

As Camilla drove away from a meeting with her investor—who, thankfully, hadn't withdrawn financial support for the restaurant after seeing all those negative social media comments about her—she saw Jordan's name appear on her phone screen. Her conflicted heart was already tearing at the seams, so she finally gave in and answered.

"Hey," she said as she pulled over to the side of the road.

"Fifth time is the charm," he replied, probably referring to the four other "missed" calls he'd made this past weekend. "How are you?"

"I'm doing okay. Just really, you know, busy right now. How are *you*?"

"Well, I'm going crazy over here not knowing what you're thinking or how you're feeling. I miss you, Camilla."

She squeezed her eyes shut. "I miss you, too."

"Then why won't you see me?"

"Because I think we both need to cool down, give each other some space, and take a little time to consider what we really want."

"Except I already know what I want. I want you."

Heat spread over her skin before a sudden chill set in. As much as she loved hearing him say the words, she knew that she had to be strong and hold her ground. "Then you'll have to wait until I figure out what *I* want."

"How long will that take?" he asked, and she could picture him looking at his watch.

"There's no timetable. This isn't something you can put on your schedule or a deadline you can write into a contract. I'm not going anywhere, Jordan. I'm just asking for some space."

"And I promise that I'm trying my hardest to give you that space." He really was, she knew. The Jordan she'd met a few weeks ago would've casually shown up everywhere he thought she might be in the hopes of spending time with her. So for him, this was progress. That didn't stop the negotiator in him from adding, "But I can't prove to you we're meant to be together if we're never actually together."

"I get it. It's just that I need to be sure you're ready for a real relationship with a woman who…" She paused, not wanting to use the same words others had used to describe her. Camilla knew who she was and refused to be defined by any of those haters on social media. "With a woman like me."

"You mean a beautiful and smart and capable woman who doesn't need me? I think I've already proven that I'm more than ready for that."

"But for how long, Jordan? How long will you be willing to put up with all the disapproval from your father and the rest of the world? Who's to say that you won't get tired of the turmoil and go back to women who fit into the mold of who a Taylor should date?"

"Neither one of us can answer that unless you give us a chance to find out," he countered. "It's like this restaurant you're planning to open, right? You've crunched all the numbers, you've analyzed all the data, you've studied all the business models. I can tell you until I'm blue in the face that it's going to be a success because I'm confident in the person running it. But the rest of the town won't know it's a success until after you open your doors and they can see it for themselves. There's no reward without risk."

"This isn't a business, though, Jordan. This is my—" Camilla cut herself off before she said the word *heart*. She wasn't ready to admit that to herself, let alone to him. "Look, it's taken me years to plan this restaurant. To, as you put it, open up my doors and take the risk. So, yeah, I'm going to want a little more time before I jump into another risk. Especially when all the cost analysis reports I've seen regarding your past dating history don't exactly show a high rate of return."

Camilla wished she could take back the words as soon as she said them. After all, Jordan had never asked for a spreadsheet on *her* dating history. She would've fumed in protest if any guy had wanted to hold her past relationships against her. Not that there were many serious ones, but there was a reason she'd never taken anyone home to meet her family before now.

"That's the difference between us, I guess," Jordan replied. "I don't see being with you as a risk."

Camilla let her head fall against the headrest. "That's because you don't really have as much to lose."

Chapter Twelve

Jordan leaned back in his desk chair, staring at the office ceiling in frustration after he got off the phone with Camilla. Then he stared at the papers on his desk until all the numbers and graphs blurred together.

"Can I be straight with you, sport?" Mac asked when she returned to the office after another coffee break and found him on the exact same page of the growth strategy report he'd been reading when she'd left.

"When are you ever *not* straight, Mac?"

She planted herself on the arm of the leather chair across from his desk. "You look like a batter in the bottom of the ninth, the bases are loaded and your team is down by three runs. You're itching to get that grand slam so bad, you're liable to swing at anything the pitcher throws your way."

He folded his hands to keep from tapping his fingers impatiently, thereby proving the accuracy of Mac's assessment. "Is this the part of the baseball analogy where you tell me it's okay to strike out?"

"Nope. This is the part where I tell you that sometimes you gotta take the walk and just get yourself on first base. Don't be so desperate to be the hero that you end up blowing the whole game."

"That's the same advice you gave me when you coached my softball team in fifth grade, Mac," Daphne said as she breezily swung into his office holding a pizza box from the Brick Oven and two plastic containers filled with salads.

"This is unexpected," Jordan told his sister, his nose lifting at the delicious scent of garlic and tomato sauce. "Does Dad know you're here?"

"Do you think I would've made it past security if Dad knew I was here? Or if he knew I was smuggling in a couple of veggie antipasto salads into the sacred halls of beef?"

"You brought me lunch?" he asked.

"Mac said you haven't been eating as well since Camilla stopped inviting you over for Sunday dinners. I guess the Sanchez family didn't like that social media piece on their daughter."

"Now that Daphne is here to coach you," Mac said as she sprang up from her seat, pushing up the long sleeves under her all-stars jersey, "I'm gonna head down to that new sporting goods shop in Billings and spend my upcoming Christmas bonus."

"You don't need any more sporting gear," he called out to Mac's back as she headed down the hallway. Then Jordan turned to his sister. "And I don't need a coach."

"Maybe not." Daphne settled herself into the chair across from him and opened the white cardboard box, sending his nostrils and his growling stomach into overdrive. "But I might have a few pointers anyway."

Jordan snorted. "How many times have you been in love, little sis?"

"Does Tiny Tim count?" she asked before sinking her teeth into a slice of cheese pizza. Her mouth was still full when her eyes went round. "Wait. Are you saying that you actually *love* Camilla?"

"I think so." The heaviness in Jordan's chest suddenly disappeared. Like he'd been holding in a breath and could finally exhale. It was such a relief to say it out loud to someone. Unfortunately, the relief was short-lived. "But even if I confessed as much to her, she'd probably doubt it anyway. She wants us to let things cool down until we can figure out what we actually want. For some reason, she thinks I'm going to change my mind down the road and call things off."

"Why would she think that?" The sarcasm dripped from Daphne's voice.

"Who knows?" Jordan shook his head, choosing to ignore his sister's tone. "What she *should* be thinking is that I'm a nice guy who cares about her and loves being with her."

"Okay, but to be fair, you're also a guy whose dating history reads like those old-timey gold mine maps they used to sell at the general store, all speculation with so many twists and turns and absolutely no depth."

"Those gold mine maps were for the tourists who didn't know any better. Just like all those ghost stories about the supposed haunted history of Bronco. People will believe anything if it's sensationalized enough. The reality, though, is that there's no comparison because I've never dated anyone like Camilla."

"She's also probably never dated anyone like you. Or at least anyone with a father like yours. Of course she's going to be wary."

"Ours," Jordan corrected as he picked up another slice. It was plain cheese, unfortunately, with no extra toppings. But at least there were pesto twists and a salad for some variety. "It's not fair for either one of us to be responsible for our dad's behavior or his opinions."

"Listen, Jordan." Daphne passed him a napkin. "I know you don't like to be compared to Dad and I don't blame you. The guy is overbearing and snobbish and an all around pain in the neck. But he's also determined and driven and isn't afraid to go after what he wants. You inherited that from him, which is great when it comes to business. But it's not so great when it comes to the people you love."

"So you're saying I shouldn't go after Camilla?"

"No. I'm saying that if you really love her—not *want* her, but *love* her—then you should sit back and give her the space that she needs. If you don't, you'll wind up pushing her away."

"But if I could just—"

"Uh-uh." Daphne waved a pizza crust at him in warning.

"I'm just saying that I could prove—"

"No." His sister drew back her arm, a throwback to her softball pitching days.

"Then how do I show her—"

Instead of the crust, Daphne switched hands and sent a balled-up napkin flying at him, clipping his chin with sauce and grease before it fell on the pile of boring reports. "This isn't about you, Jordan. It's about her. When you read through all those comments under that picture of the two of you kissing, were any of them negative about you?"

He sat back in his chair, the pizza weighing heavily in his stomach as he thought about some of the rude things people had said about Camilla. "You're right. She bore the brunt of it. I think there were only a handful that implied I was thinking with my—"

Daphne launched a cherry tomato at him this time to cut him off. "That's still not an insult to *you*, Jordan. It might sound like it at first, but what they're really saying is that your attraction to her can only be related to sex because she has nothing else to offer you."

"But that's not true," he all but shouted at the ceiling for what felt like the millionth time. He rolled his neck to loosen up the coiled muscles in his shoulders. "Camilla Sanchez is one of the most amazing women I've ever met. She has more to offer me than I could ever offer her."

"Then be patient and wait for her to offer it."

Daphne left after they finished eating and Jordan found himself even more restless than he'd been before. He'd never been very good at just sitting back and being patient.

He got through another few hours of paperwork before deciding to let off some steam by going for a run. Mac, being a firm believer in taking breaks from work to exercise, always insisted he keep a supply of athletic clothes and sneakers in his executive washroom.

Normally, Jordan would have run along the hilly terrain toward his ranch, but since the sun was already going down, he took off toward the more populated area of Bronco Heights.

A massive pine tree had already been erected in the park in front of City Hall and festive lights were strung up all over town. Most of the local businesses had decorated their storefronts with a combination of garlands, wreaths and themed window displays. He passed several restaurants with signs out front telling customers to "reserve your holiday meals now."

One restaurant he didn't pass, though, was DJ's Deluxe. In fact, he crossed the street as he neared the renovated building because he didn't want to be tempted with the thought of looking in the windows to catch a glimpse of Camilla.

Even the popular Bronco Ghost Tours seemed to be getting into the holiday spirit with a sandwich board sign outside its office offering special "Yuletide" programs. He wasn't even sure what a yuletide was. Jordan had never really participated in any of the historical traditions involving Christmas, unless he counted Santa Claus. And really, Santa had only come to his house depending on the stepmother at the time. Or unless one of his uncles dressed up for a charity event.

Normally, his family focused on the business aspect of the holiday because that was when their biggest orders came in. The only tradition that stayed the same was the huge company party for the Taylor Beef employees where his father passed out hefty bonuses.

Jessica had ordered personalized stockings this year, though. Including one for Daphne, which their father hadn't yet taken down from the fireplace mantle. So maybe some things would be changing this December.

As usual, someone had driven their plow to town and pushed the most recently fallen snow into a small hill at one end of the park where neighborhood kids could bring out their sleds and safely race each other down the man-made slopes.

By this time of the evening, everyone was off work and out of school and families were out in full force with colorful knitted scarves and mittens, enjoying the wintertime activities while happy couples moved in and out of the brightly lit shops. It seemed as though the entire town was already preparing for the most wonderful time of the year.

Everyone except for him.

Jordan zigzagged down several residential

blocks, yet each time he turned onto another street, he found his way back toward the center of town. He tried to focus on the short bursts of condensation in the cold wintry air as his breathing came faster and harder. Unfortunately, all he could see were decorations and lights and sleds and the excitement of the season surrounding him.

On Thanksgiving, he'd actually envisioned himself spending Christmas with the Sanchez family, but that was probably out of the question. With Camilla freezing him out and his own family so fractured and dysfunctional right now, where would Jordan even spend the holiday this year?

Mac had always welcomed him with open arms and Daphne might want to host something out at Happy Hearts, so maybe he had options. But not the one he wanted.

After a few laps around the park, Jordan returned to the street and slowed as he passed the decorated displays in the store windows. He would have to get presents for his sister and his assistant, and whoever else he ended up spending the holiday with. When he got to the window display at Playworks, he paused to watch an electric train zoom around the toys inside.

A plush pink pig that looked almost identical to Tiny Tim caught his eye. It would be a perfect gift for Camilla if he wasn't trying to get her to take him seriously. He glanced over his shoulder at the jewelry store across the street. If he really wanted to cause a stir, he'd head over there and give everyone something to talk about. But he didn't want to make things worse for Camilla.

Returning his gaze to the window display of toys, his eyes landed on a porcelain doll in a red velvet dress, which reminded him that Erica Abernathy had just had a baby and he hadn't bought the child a gift yet. Perhaps it was a sign. Or at least an excuse.

Opening the shop door and stepping foot in such an establishment went against every one of Jordan's natural instincts. But then again, so did buying a woman a stuffed pig.

When Erica answered the door, Jordan immediately noticed the smudged circles under her eyes and the impossible-to-contain smile across her face. "Hey, Jordan! Did someone from human resources send more paperwork for me to fill out?"

When Erica had moved back to Bronco a couple of months ago, she'd needed a job. She'd come to see Jordan as a last resort and it had been easy enough to find her a position at Taylor Beef where she could start after the baby was born. In the meantime, she'd met and married Morgan Dalton and was now living at his house out on Dalton's Grange. The Daltons were relatively new to Bronco, but Jordan had been to their ranch before to check out some of their livestock.

He held up the pale yellow bag. "No, I brought a gift."

"But you already sent the wine basket when I was in the hospital. I couldn't drink it because my milk was already coming in, but the nurses all loved it."

Jordan winced at his mistake. Maybe he needed to come up with a get-well gift that was a little less one-size-fits-all. "This one is for the baby, though. Is she here?"

Erica put a shushing finger to her lips before standing to the side of the door to let him inside. "Come on in. Morgan is trying to get Josie back to sleep right now."

"Oh, I don't want to bother you guys. I just wanted to drop this off." He passed the bag to her.

"You're not bothering us at all." She walked toward the living room, leaving him to follow as she pulled tissue paper out of the bag.

"The sales clerk said that it's for toddlers," Jordan explained as he took a seat on the leather sofa opposite her stuffed rocking chair. "So you might have to wait another month or so to give it to her."

"Jordan, how old do you think a toddler is supposed to be?" Erica shook her head, yet kept smiling as she studied the box containing miniature horses and cows and action figures. "Oh, it's a My First Rodeo Set. That's pretty cute considering this is probably *your* first rodeo buying a baby gift."

Jordan cleared his throat. "The past month has been a bunch of firsts for me, actually."

"So I've read online."

"Speaking of Camilla…" He squirmed slightly in his seat. "Can I ask you a question?"

"Jordan, you were the only person in town willing to hire an eight-months-pregnant lady without any references from my previous employer. And you insisted I didn't have to start until after the baby arrived. I think you've earned the right to ask me anything you want."

"What was it like for you when we dated?" he asked, then saw the tilt of her head and quickly corrected himself. "I know that sounds kind of awkward since you're happily married and your husband is in the other room. But I'm asking from a data analysis standpoint."

"No, I know what you meant. I'm just trying to figure out how to say this in the most polite way possible."

"Don't sugarcoat it." He leaned forward, putting his forearms on his knees as though he was ready to take notes.

"Well, it was over ten years ago and we only went out a handful of times. I had just graduated high school and both of our families were putting all that pressure on us despite the fact that we both knew we weren't right for each other. But…"

"But?"

Erica studied him for a few seconds before saying, "But I remember thinking that it was very sad that you would never know when you found *the one* because you never really spent any time with a woman long enough to figure it out. You always seemed to be looking over your shoulder."

He jerked his head back. "Like I was afraid of something?"

"No, like you were looking for something better to come along."

He scratched at the back of his neck, as though he could scrub away the mistakes of his past. "It might've seemed that way. But it wasn't how I meant it."

"Jordan, you literally told me not to get attached to the first guy I met when I got to college. In fact, I believe your exact words were 'There'll always be someone else around the corner, kid.'"

Okay, so maybe that wasn't the best philosophy to instill in an impressionable teenager. But in his defense, he'd been young too, and determined not to make the same mistakes in love that his father had made.

"Well, it seems like you held out for the right guy." He jerked his thumb toward the framed wedding photo of her and Morgan.

"That's the thing, though. Morgan came into my life when I least expected it." Erica's eyes went from tired to sparkling. "When I was no longer looking around any corners, so to speak. See, it doesn't matter how many other women are out there waiting for you, Jordan, if you refuse to settle down long enough to give the right woman a fair shot."

"Okay, I might've been that way ten years ago. Or even ten weeks ago. But now I've actually found the one. My problem is that I haven't been able to convince her that I'm the one *for her*."

"And you're used to convincing people into anything," Erica replied, repeating what everyone else had already been saying about him.

"What is up with people always jumping to that conclusion about me?" Jordan asked.

"Sorry to interrupt, babe." Morgan came out of the hallway cradling a little bundle wrapped in blankets. "Josie wants nothing to do with her crib. I have a feeling she recognized the voice of the man who sprang into action when her mama went into labor and cleared all those partygo-ers out of the way like he was culling a herd of cattle."

"Here, I'll take her." Erica held out her arms for the baby, whose eyes were round and alert.

Jordan stood up to shake Morgan's hand. "Sorry for barging in like this. I wanted to drop off a gift."

Erica pulled a pink blanket off the ottoman beside her so Morgan could take a seat. "I was just about to tell Jordan that he can't convince Camilla he is the one for her. He's going to have to wait for her to come to that conclusion on her own." She turned back to face Jordan. "If it's meant to be, you guys will find your way back to each other."

"What do you think, Josie?" Jordan asked the baby girl in Erica's arms, who was staring at him with curiosity. "Do you think I should just give up on the woman I love?"

"No!" both Erica and Morgan said loudly in unison, causing the baby to pinch her tiny face into a startled expression.

"Sorry for sounding so adamant," Erica said, then murmured reassuringly until her daughter's face softened again. "It's just that we're witness-ing firsthand what happens when someone gives up on the love of their life."

Jordan glanced between Erica and Morgan,

who by all appearances seemed to be completely smitten with each other.

"No, not us," Morgan clarified. "Erica's grandfather, Josiah."

"Oh, I heard he's out at Snowy Mountain Senior Care. Do they let them have girlfriends there?"

"No, Gramps was in love with a woman named Winona seventy-five years ago. We found his journal where he talked about how they had a baby girl named Beatrix, who was given up for adoption against his wishes."

"I think I heard about this." Jordan snapped his fingers. "One of the customers at Camilla's mom's beauty shop was talking about some missing baby. She mentioned the Abernathys being involved, but I didn't realize it was your grandfather."

"Probably because you never pay attention to social media. My brother, Gabe, his fiancée, Melanie, and I have launched a nationwide search for Beatrix, who might be going by the name Daisy now. Anyway, my point is that Gramps totally regretted giving up on Winona and losing track of her and their baby. Don't be like Gramps."

"Okay, but you just told me *not* to try and convince Camilla to be with me." Jordan scrubbed his hands over his face in exasperation. "If I'm not trying, then I pretty much *am* giving up."

Erica sighed as if it should be so obvious. "She doesn't need to be convinced to be with you. Camilla will figure that out all on her own as long as she knows that you're not going to take off running at the first opportunity."

"If I was in your boots, which I was not too long ago—" Morgan smirked at him before giving a pointed nod toward the ring on Erica's finger "—I'd make sure that the woman I loved knew I was committed to being with her for the long haul."

Erica turned to her husband and kissed him warmly, making Jordan miss Camilla all the more. Baby Josie also stirred in her mother's arms, as though trying to remind her parents they weren't the only two people in the room.

"Well, I should probably get going. I hope you guys find this missing relative. And I hope *you*," Jordan said as he pointed to the sweet little face peering at him from her nest of blankets, "enjoy your first rodeo set. But apparently not until you're a little bit older."

Josie made a cooing noise as Jordan stood up to leave, and the charming sound echoed in his ears as he drove away from the Dalton ranch. The momentary pang bouncing around his chest was unexpected and different from any of the other pangs of loneliness he'd been experiencing lately. This one wasn't because of the story of Josiah's lost love or even the threat of Jordan losing his own love if Camilla decided she didn't want him.

This pang was due to that adorable bundle in Erica's arms and that sweet cooing sound and the thought that Jordan might never have a baby of his own.

Whoa.

Where had that thought come from? He'd never so much as bought a baby gift, let alone been around an actual baby. In fact, he'd never given more than a passing thought to the idea of having children, yet suddenly he was envisioning all the babies he wanted to have.

With Camilla.

Slow down, he told himself, glancing in his review mirror as though the baby patrol was right behind him. Having kids was still a ways down the road. But just the thought of building a relationship with Camilla—building a real future with her—made him envision the life he hadn't known he wanted. Love, partnership and eventually a family.

Unfortunately, he still wasn't any closer to convincing Camilla of their future together.

Chapter Thirteen

Camilla officially finished her last shift at DJ's Deluxe on the first Friday in December. She'd purposely chosen one of the busiest nights of the week so that her coworkers wouldn't be able to make a big deal or throw her some sort of farewell party. But then DJ had talked her into working Saturday night selling hot cocoa and beef sliders at the food booth during the annual tree lighting ceremony in the park. Since everyone in the Sanchez family usually volunteered at the various booths during community events, and since people would have made even more suspicious assumptions about Camilla if she didn't attend, she'd grudgingly agreed.

But her heart wasn't in it. In fact, her heart wasn't into anything lately.

Just as she was clocking out for the final time, one of the bussers came into the office upstairs and said, "Hey, Camilla, there's a guy waiting for you in the bar."

Her heart fluttered inside her chest and she thought, *Finally*. She'd told Jordan to give her more time, but that hadn't stopped her from expecting him to show up at the restaurant like he had after they'd first met. The man didn't give up so easily no matter what anyone said.

This past week, Camilla should've been glad that he was following her wishes. However, as each shift had gone by and he hadn't so much as made a takeout order, she'd begun to think that maybe he'd already gotten over her more quickly than they'd both expected.

But now he was downstairs in the bar. A thrill of excitement shot through her, and she stopped by the employee break room to check her appearance in the mirror and maybe run a little bit of gloss over her lips. She shuddered when she saw her reflection, though. Her hair was in a lopsided bun, her shirt was a wrinkled mess, and her red-rimmed eyes suggested she hadn't slept in days. Overall, she looked about as miserable as she felt. Probably because she'd been burning the candle at both ends, trying to stay busy so she wouldn't have to think about Jordan.

She fixed her hair, then eagerly descended the steps to the main floor, taking a deep breath and preparing herself for what she would say when she finally saw him. Yet instead of seeing Jordan waiting for her at the bar, it was her father.

"Don't look so disappointed to see me, *mija*," Aaron Sanchez said as he spread open his arms.

Camilla was wound so tightly with so many different emotions, she fell into his embrace. As he wrapped her in a bear hug, she experienced all the warm comfort of her childhood right here in the bar of the busiest restaurant in town. When she finally pulled back, she explained, "I'm not disappointed, Dad. I was just expecting it to be someone else."

"Still haven't talked to that Taylor boy, eh?" Dad patted the bar stool beside him, then asked Leo the bartender to bring them both a glass of the Chateau Montelena. This must be serious if Dad was ordering one of the most expensive chardonnays in DJ's fine wine cellars.

"He called me last week, but to be fair, I *did* tell him I needed some space."

Her father nodded. "It's good that he's respecting your wishes."

"That's what Mom told me, too. Which is weird because I thought you guys liked Jordan."

"Oh, we like him just fine. But if you don't want him, then we're not going to try and talk you into being with a man just because *we* bonded with him."

Leo placed the two chilled glasses in front of them, and Camilla had to wait forever while her dad first sampled the wine, then nodded for the bartender pour it.

"How could you have bonded with him, Dad?" She took an unladylike gulp as soon as Leo left. "You barely even know him."

"Know him? *Mija*, I've sorted and shipped and delivered all the mail in this town for how many years now? You know who knows the most about the residents?"

"The mail carrier." She recited the answer ingrained in her since childhood, and was recently reminded of during Thanksgiving. All her life, her father let it be known to his family that he delivered the most personal information to people's houses every day.

"Exactly. I know who gets letters from the IRS and who gets those magazines that come in brown wrappers. I know who belongs to which political parties and who tries to reuse the same stamps over again because they need every cent."

"Is this where you tell me all of Jordan Taylor's secrets?"

"If he had any, yes." Dad clinked his glass against hers before taking another sip and swishing it around his mouth slowly, as if he was at a leisurely wine tasting event. Camilla could've finished an entire bottle in the amount of time it took him to finally continue. "Instead, this is where I tell you that I also know all the good stuff about him."

"Like what?" Camilla asked, a regular glutton for punishment. The man had likely given up on her by now, and learning about the one she let get away was bound to only depress her more.

"Like he gets personally addressed letters from countless charities—the kind you usually only receive if you make big donations. The humane society, Girls in Science, scholarships for local kids, as well as kids all over the world. You know, all the organizations ol' Cornelius doesn't give to because it doesn't involve a flashy gala where he is the center of attention."

"Don't knock the fancy galas, Dad. I've been to one and it actually raised an obscene amount of money."

Her father continued as though he didn't hear her. "Jordan also sends his former nanny a box of her favorite chocolates and a card every year, I assume for her birthday. And she sends him one in return. He has a pen pal through the Best Buddies program *and* the Wounded Warriors

Foundation, and their letters go out and come in like clockwork. Plus, it's no secret he mails off a check every month subsidizing the owner of those batting cages over by the Bronco Little League field so that competitive assistant of his is always guaranteed her favorite fast pitch machine. Should I go on?"

Camilla's shoulders sank lower with every example her dad relayed as proof of Jordan's upstanding character. "I know he is a good man, Dad. I mean, I knew he was willing to volunteer for all those local events with me. I guess I just didn't realize he'd been doing those kinds of good deeds all along."

"Probably because you were like everyone else and stayed blinded by what they wrote about him in the society pages and on social media."

"It's not that I didn't know he was capable of it. It's just that I also wasn't looking for reasons to fall in love with him any more than I already am."

"So you *are* in love with him." Her dad let out a deep breath. "Your mother said that might be the reason why you're pushing him away."

"Who says I'm pushing anyone away?" Camilla asked, knowing full well it was exactly what she was doing. She preferred thinking of it as giving Jordan time to figure out how he felt about her. But really, she knew she was just giving him the reason he probably needed to break things off and go his own way.

"Because you did the same thing when you were in high school and that geography teacher wanted everyone to do those reports about a country. You spent days working on that report about Mexico and then you gave a presentation in class about the culture and had to bring in a food item from that region. Remember we got those recipes from your *tio* Marco and you were supposed to bring all the ingredients to class and then show everyone how to make *birria*?"

"I thought I made quesadillas for that report." Camilla swallowed her feelings with another gulp of wine.

"You did. You took in grated cheese and those store-bought tortillas and melted it together in a pan when it was your turn to present. You were afraid that if you got up in front of the class and tried to make what you really wanted, you'd mess it up and everyone would say you weren't truly Mexican. And to be honest with you, there was probably no way you could've pulled off that recipe. At least not on Mr. Watanabe's portable stovetop and that microwave he borrowed from the science teacher."

She narrowed her eyes. "I seem to recall you being a little more supportive of that presentation back in high school."

Her father threw up his hands. "Of course I told you that you could do it, even though it took you at least five times practicing at home before you finally got it right. But you were so afraid of messing up, of being laughed at, that you gave up and went the easy route."

"Is there a point to this story other than reminding me about my hopeless cooking skills?"

He took a much bigger drink of his wine this time, as though his own patience were also coming to an end. "My point is that you should've made the *birria*. Even if it wasn't perfect, it still would've been more authentic than those quesadillas. Just like you should try and make things work with Jordan. Even if the relationship ends up being a disaster, at least it would be authentic because you're being true to yourself."

Camilla set her elbows on the polished bar top as she massaged her temples. "What if it's too late to make things work with Jordan?"

"Why would you think it's too late?" her dad asked.

"Because you and Mom were right and I probably did push him away. I was afraid that if I fell for him and he ended up leaving, it would hurt too much."

"What would hurt? Your heart or your reputation?"

Camilla drew in a ragged breath. "Both."

"Maybe. But you won't know unless you give it a shot." Her dad tucked his hand under her chin and lifted her face until she was staring at the unwavering love reflected in his eyes. "Plus the poor guy is so *crazy* about you that he and Felix actually lost last weekend's basketball game to Dante and Dylan. Your brothers have no intention of letting him live it down, either."

"Wait." Camilla sat up straighter on her bar stool. She'd purposely avoided going to her parents' house because she didn't want them asking questions about what was going on with him. Had she missed something? "Jordan came over for Sunday night dinner?"

"Not for dinner because he said he was trying to respect your space. But when Felix called him to see if he could still shoot some hoops, he couldn't get there quick enough. Mom was upset that you weren't there, by the way. You never miss family dinners so she's been worried about you. She tried to ask Jordan what was going on, but he kept pretty tight-lipped."

"Good," Camilla said, though something in her heart suddenly felt much lighter. If Jordan had gone to see her family a few days ago, then he hadn't really given up on her. "You guys are all too nosy and need to learn how to mind your own business."

"You kids *are* our business." He finished the

remainder of his wine, then pulled some cash out of his wallet and left it on the bar.

It was then that Camilla noticed the knee cart wheeled up against the other side of his stool. She looked down at the soft cast on his foot as he scooted forward, then she scanned the waiting area. "Dad, did you get the okay to drive out here?"

"No, your mom drove us. She sent me in here to talk to you since I'm the family referee."

Camilla followed her father out of the restaurant, pulling on her puffy down coat as they went toward the end of the street where the employees parked. "So if you've got referee duty tonight, then what is Mom doing?"

"She's running the scouting report." Her dad held open the car door for her. "Your mom overheard Sofia talking about meeting some new guy at the Brick Oven, so she's stationed over there to check him out. I'm going to meet her there."

Apparently, Cornelius Taylor wasn't the only over-protective parent in town. Just one more thing she and Jordan had in common.

"Are you and mom going to tell the others about this potential boyfriend?" Camilla sank into the driver's seat, her aching feet tingling with relief. "Or are you going to wait until Christmas dinner for everyone to find out like you guys did with Jordan?"

"We'll see if this new one lasts that long." Her father shut the door, then gave one last wave as he scooted away.

Camilla sat in her car as the heater came to life.

The shops and restaurants of Bronco were in full holiday mode with lights and decorations and even a dusting of snow along the sidewalk. December in Bronco was the most magical time of the year and an hour ago, Camilla hadn't exactly been feeling the holiday spirit.

But finding out that Jordan was still interested in her suddenly made everything shine brighter. It certainly made her heart feel lighter. She just needed to figure out a way to make things right with him.

Maybe she should remind him that, according to their original agreement, they still had one date left.

On the first Saturday of December, all the local merchants and craft vendors came together to sponsor the Bronco Tree Lighting Ceremony at the park in front of City Hall. It was one of Camilla's favorite traditions, and nobody in her family would even consider putting up their own decorations or buying so much as a stocking stuffer until the town tree was officially lit.

Camilla also knew it would be the perfect

place to talk to Jordan. She was the one who'd been so insistent on keeping their relationship private, so it was up to her to prove that she would be willing to finally take things public. And what better place to do that than at Bronco's most public event of the year?

Working in DJ's booth on the side serving hot cocoas, Camilla had a perfect view of the enormous tree and the stage erected in the town square. First the mayor would speak and introduce all the council members, and then various dignitaries and community leaders would all stand around patting each other on the back. This year, Dante's class was the winner of the annual Christmas carol contest and would be performing on stage right before the grand tree marshal (similar to a parade grand marshal) led the countdown before flipping the switch that turned on the lights.

The white folding chairs in front of the stage were usually reserved for town VIPs, so she easily spotted Jessica and Cornelius Taylor and a couple of gentlemen who were probably Jordan's uncles. She saw several people from the Abernathy clan with them, as well as Daniel DuBois, who was sitting with his wife, Brittany, and their ten-month old, Hailey.

Amanda Jenkins was in the crowd with her fiancé, Holt Dalton, and his parents and brothers. Holt's son Robby had actually been one of the first customers when the hot cocoa stand opened.

So many wealthy ranchers and notable towns-people were in attendance tonight, it was hard to keep track.

Camilla waved at Daphne in between orders and even caught a glimpse of Daphne's brother Brandon with a couple of his Taylor cousins.

The only Taylor she hadn't seen so far this evening was Jordan.

Maybe he knew she would be there working at the booth and he was still trying to give her space. Camilla's brain wanted to be happy that he was willing to do what she wanted, but her heart was in a flurry as she searched out every dark-haired man that passed by her booth.

However, her plan to talk to him soon lost traction as she realized he might not show. As the night wore on, the speeches were made, the carol was sung, the tree was lit, and everyone in the park let out a roaring cheer. And still no Jordan.

Camilla was vacillating between frustra-tion and regret as she continued to pass out hot cocoa, one after the next, averting her eyes from the customers—many of whom were her neigh-bors and friends—until she heard a very famil-iar voice.

"Do you have any toppings to go with the hot cocoa?" Jordan's dimples flickered in the twinkling lights, but Camilla could also see the vulnerability written all over his face.

He was here. Standing in front of her. Making her pulse race with excitement. And all she could think to say was, "Um, we've got whipped cream and chocolate syrup. We might still have some marshmallows left."

"Great. I'll take all of them."

"Of course you will," she said, unable to contain the smile spreading across her face. "You're all about the extras."

"I'm here purely as a customer," he said, and her stomach dropped.

"Oh." She paused long enough to blink back the disappointment. Then she transferred the steamed milk into the to-go cup.

"I mean, I'm here to see you, obviously. But I know you're working. I was going to wait until later, but I started getting cold and thought you wouldn't mind serving me if I was at your booth for legitimate reasons. Anyway, I just wanted you to know that I'd like to talk to you when you're done, but I understand if you'd rather do it another time."

"Leo, can you take over for me?" Camilla asked her coworker manning the cash register.

Then she handed Jordan the cup and said, "I'll be right out."

Shuddering with excitement, she didn't bother with her purse, but managed to grab a scarf before meeting Jordan outside the booth.

"Hey," he said, almost tentatively. She hated that she'd been the one to make him doubt himself around her.

"Hi," she replied.

"Maybe we should go somewhere private and talk?" he asked.

"Actually, I was hoping to get a close-up view of the tree."

"But there are people around." He glanced sideways at her.

She took his hand and pulled him forward. "Jordan, there will always be people around."

His smile returned with its full force, and her knees reminded her that she hadn't grown immune to the flooding sensation of Jordan flashing those straight white teeth at her.

As they neared the stage area, which now featured a quintet of singers dressed in Victorian costumes and singing "O Come, All Ye Faithful," she asked, "So what did you want to talk to me about?"

He cleared his throat. "I'm not sorry that I mistook you for someone else at the Denim and Diamonds gala because it led me to go searching for who you really are. And I'm definitely not sorry that I talked you into letting me take you out on those dates. But I *am* sorry that I might've come on too strong at first and I'm sorry that my father can be a pain in the ass and I'm especially sorry that I put you in the position where people questioned who you were and why we were together." Jordan paused long enough to draw in a deep breath before soldiering on. "I can't change who I am. I'm always going to be a Taylor and gossip is always going to follow me. I know that dealing with all of that is a lot to ask of you and, believe me, I wouldn't ask if I wasn't one hundred percent sure that it wouldn't be worth it for you in the end. Because I love you, Camilla Sanchez, and you're the only woman I will ever want. So whether it takes six dates or six years or six decades, I will be here waiting to prove myself to you."

Jordan had just told her he loved her. Her heart felt as though it was lifting off in that private helicopter of his, soaring in the sky above the mountains and looking down at her and the view of this amazing man in front of her who had never backed away from a challenge. Camilla didn't think she could be any happier.

Still. She had her own plan of what she wanted to say to him and just because he was surprising her by pledging his love first didn't mean that she wasn't going to tell him exactly how she felt. After all, one of the major rules in a negotiation was to always be ready with a counteroffer.

"Five," she corrected him.

Jordan scrunched his brow in confusion.

"We agreed on six, but we've only had five dates," she clarified. "You still owe me one more."

"Well, if we're going by our original dating rules," he said as he held up the cup of warm milk she'd given him before even bothering to add the cocoa mix, "I'm going to need more of a substantial meal than this."

"Done," she said, taking the cup from his hand before tossing it in the nearby trash bin.

Then she planted her hands on the front of his jacket, pulled him closer to her and said, "Right after I get my kiss."

Chapter Fourteen

Camilla was kissing him. Right here in front of the entire town, and likely their cameras. And Jordan had never been more willing or determined to be a public spectacle in his whole life.

He wrapped his arms around her waist and slid his hands underneath the hem of her coat, relishing the taste of her mouth. It had been a little over a week but he'd already missed the feel of her in his arms.

When he pulled back, he smiled down at her upturned face. "That was a hello kiss, not a good-bye one, right?"

"It was more of an 'I'm sorry' kiss," she replied. "It was unfair of me to let my own fears get in the way of us trying to make this relationship work. I love you, Jordan, and I never should have held back on my feelings."

Her words hit him with a force and his knees nearly buckled as his chest expanded. "You love me?"

"Of course I do." She held his face in her palms, but she might as well have been holding his heart. "I usually pride myself on being so passionate and forthcoming and at ease when it comes to everything else in my life. The night I met you, I was all of those things because I didn't think I had anything to lose. But as soon as I started to feel something for you, I held myself back because I got scared."

"You had every right to be wary, though. I know my track record and I know my family." He jerked his chin to where Cornelius was standing with the mayor in front of the kettle corn booth hosted by the Future Farmers of America. Jordan's father didn't look too pleased by his son's very public display of affection, but the old man better get used to it. He turned back to Camilla. "I promised not to pressure you or push you into making any decisions. And even though you just openly admitted that you loved me in front of basically the whole town, I'll still give you as much time as you need. As long as you know that I'm not giving up."

"Even if it won't be easy?" Camilla asked. Her arms were still loosely draped around his shoulders, proving that she clearly wasn't willing to give up, either.

"Few things worth having are easy. I knew I loved you after our first week together and I'm not going to stop just because things get hard. You should know by now that when things get tough, I only dig my heels in deeper."

Camilla threw back her head to laugh, the musical sound making Jordan feel a million feet tall. "Well, my family is heading over this way, so you better be sure that this is what you want."

"What I really want is to spend this Christmas with you. And every Christmas after that. If that's what *you* want."

Camilla's lips quivered and she blinked several times. "Are you asking what I think you're asking?"

"Not if it will scare you off." Jordan held up his palms. "I'm not rushing you. I'm just saying that when you're ready, I'm ready." He reached into his pocket and pulled out a small box wrapped in gold foil paper and tied with a red Christmas bow. "You don't have to open it now. It could be a Valentine's gift, or a Fourth of July gift, or even a gift for Halloween fifty years from now. Just put it under your tree and open it whenever you're ready. Or whenever you need a reminder of the night we first met. But I'll give you a hint. It's not denim."

Camilla's eyes sparkled and she twisted her bottom lip between her teeth as she stared at the box in his outstretched hand. Finally, she lifted a corner of her mouth and asked, "What if I wanted to open my Christmas gift a little bit early?"

Camilla's fingers were practically shaking as she tore off the wrapping paper. Her eyes grew damp as she saw the familiar logo of Beaumont and Rossi's Fine Jewels on the lid. Before she knew it, Jordan took the velvet box from her trembling hand and dropped down to one knee. Camilla's stomach dropped as well when she saw the sparkling diamond ring blink up at her.

Then his words made everything else drop.

"Your smile is the first thing I want to see every morning and the last thing I want to see before I fall asleep every night. You have opened my eyes to a whole new world and a whole new way of living life, and I love the person that I've become when I'm with you. You are the most incredible and refreshing and smart and authentic woman I have ever met. Camilla Sanchez, I would be honored if you chose to make me the crown prince of your heart."

Joy radiated like a spiral from the tips of Camilla's toes all the way to her cheeks, which couldn't stretch any more to contain her grin. She heard the clicking shutters of several nearby cameras, but for the first time, she truly didn't care what anyone thought.

Nodding eagerly, she pulled the leather glove off her hand so that Jordan could slide the ring over her finger. When he stood up, he lifted her with him and swung her around as his mouth claimed hers, her body now as weightless as her floating heart.

Several cheers and a few claps on her back caused them to finally break the kiss. Jordan set her back on her feet so they could meet the crowd of people who'd circled around them.

"Congratulations, *mija*!" Her mom wrapped her in a hug. Then her parents switched out and, as her dad hugged her, Denise embraced Jordan. "Welcome to the family. Officially."

"I told you she'd come around," her father said as he shook Jordan's hand.

"Did you know about this?" she asked her parents.

"Of course they did," Sofia said before congratulating them. "When Jordan came to get their blessing, I insisted on going with him to the jewelers. After all, I picked out the dress that caused him to fall in love with you. It was only right that I help him pick out the ring." Sofia lowered her voice before whispering in Camilla's ear. "I also made sure it cost a fortune so that all the gossips couldn't miss it on those social media posts."

The sound of a throat clearing rather dramatically caused the normally exuberant Sanchez family members to go suddenly quiet. However, even the disapproving expression on Cornelius Taylor's face couldn't dampen her mood.

"Hey, Dad, you remember Camilla?" Jordan lifted her hand in his so that the engagement ring reflected in the lights of the giant Christmas tree, as well as in the calculated gleam of Cornelius Taylor's eyes. "This is her family."

"Is that so?" his father asked through his clenched jaw.

"Oh, Cornelius and I go way back." Aaron Sanchez reached out his hand first. A camera flashed, causing the senior Taylor to revert into his public persona mode and at least pretend to politely return the handshake. Camilla's dad used the opportunity to pull Cornelius in closer as he lowered his voice. "I'm the mail carrier who knows about all those letters that come back to you marked Return to Sender."

Camilla's ears perked up at that revelation, but Cornelius pasted that phony smile on his face just before another camera shutter clicked.

He spoke through his gritted teeth as he said, "Jordan, I hope you know what you're doing."

"Dad, I've spent all of my life proving to you that I know exactly what I'm doing. Now, you can either add another offspring to your ever-growing list of children who refuse to speak to you or you can finally swallow your pride, congratulate me and welcome my charming fiancée to our family."

Camilla's chest flooded with pride as Jordan placed a protective arm around her shoulders.

This time when Cornelius cleared his throat, it wasn't so much for attention as it was to help him force out the words. "Congratulations, son. Miss Sanchez, I'm sure that you will make a very lovely bride."

It wasn't a hearty welcome to the family such as the one Jordan had received from the San-chezes, but at least the older man hadn't said anything about prenuptial agreements. Yet.

"Thank you, sir." Camilla smiled with as much grace as she could muster. She used a little less grace when she purposely lifted her left hand to waggle her fingers in a wave at Jordan's stepmother as she approached the group. "Hey, Jessica."

"Is that from Beaumont and Rossi?" Jessica gave an excited little clap. "Let me see."

This brought another round of oohs and ahhs

from several women who gathered around. When one of the city council members came over to see what was going on, Cornelius puffed out his chest and spoke as though he were on the stage behind them. "Obviously, we'll have the reception out at the ranch. We'll use Brittany Brandt Dubois again for the wedding planning since she did such a great job with the gala—"

"Dad." Jordan held up his palm like a stop sign. "Just a word of warning in case you haven't already noticed. Camilla prefers to make her own decisions and you probably shouldn't try to force her into—"

"I'd be honored to have the reception at the ranch," Camilla interrupted. "After all, that's where Jordan and I first met. As long as you don't have a problem with my new restaurant catering the event."

Cornelius raised a slick silver eyebrow, and for the first time ever, Camilla saw the hint of an authentic smirk that was very similar to Jordan's. "Will this new restaurant of yours be using Taylor Beef exclusively?"

"If we can negotiate a fair price, I will be," Camilla challenged, and Jordan laughed.

"Mr. Taylor, I'm Denise Sanchez, Camilla's mother." Mom suddenly linked her arm through Cornelius's, making him do a double take at the petite mahogany-haired woman who'd suddenly appeared. "I'm noticing that your hair is in desperate need of some updating. Come into my salon next week and I'll give you the family discount."

"That would be great," Jessica interjected quickly, for once oblivious to her husband's sudden frown. She looped her arm through Cornelius's free one and, along with Camilla's mom, steered him away, saying, "I've been trying to get him to change it up a bit."

Camilla stifled a giggle, and Jordan's eyes shone with amazement. "See? A little change is exactly what my family needed."

She snuggled in closer under his arm. "And you, Jordan Taylor, are exactly what I need."

Instead of having him to herself, though, Camilla got her first experience of what it would be like as the wife of one of the most powerful and well-known businessmen in town. She could barely remember half of the names of the people who introduced themselves and offered their congratulations.

The one person, though, who didn't make their way over to wish them well was Jordan's sister, Daphne.

After shaking hands and being slapped on the back by almost everyone in town, Jordan finally turned to Camilla and asked, "Do you think the hot cocoa booth is closed yet? I never got all my toppings."

"Come on." His new fiancée's smile lit up brighter than the Christmas tree in the middle of the park. "I'll buy you one."

As they were arguing over who would pay for his drink, Daphne walked up to them. "Hey, guys, I heard the news, but didn't want to come over while Dad was around and risk causing a scene."

"You guys still haven't talked, huh?" he asked his sister, whose smile didn't quite meet her eyes.

"Nope. But don't worry about it. Tonight is all about you guys. I'm so happy my big brother is finally settling down with a woman who will keep him in check." There was a hint of sadness in her eyes before her gaze shifted to the snow flurries coming from the sky. Daphne shivered. "Anyway, you guys are very lucky to have found each other. Not everyone gets that."

"Don't worry, sis. I'm sure you'll meet someone special soon."

"I don't know if you've noticed, Jordan, but most of the ranchers around here aren't going to fall for the vegetarian of the notorious Taylor family. It doesn't matter, though." Daphne shrugged, her tone practically resigned. "I've got my animals and they've got me. Speaking of which, I have to go home for the evening feedings. Congratulations, guys."

They both gave Daphne a hug. After she left, Jordan was about to ask Camilla if she thought his sister seemed a little off, but he didn't get the chance because they were next in line.

"Have you told him the big secret?" Mac asked Camilla before handing Jordan a hot cocoa with all the toppings. Apparently, there were now two women in this world who knew what he wanted before he even asked.

"What big secret?" he asked cautiously. "And why are you working at the DJ's Deluxe booth, Mac?"

"I wanted to get some experience in the food industry before our grand opening," his assistant said.

Jordan took too big of a gulp and scalded his tongue. He hissed as his mouth drew in a few pants of cold air. "What grand opening?"

Camilla squeezed his hand. "Mac is my silent partner."

"What?" Jordan looked between the two women, unsure if he could handle any more surprises today. "When did this happen?"

"When I ran into Camilla over at the U of Montana. One of my players is being scouted by a club team over there and we got to talking about the college campus. You know," Mac said as she leaned against the table, ignoring the line of people behind them, "if U of M woulda had a softball team back in my day, I'd have gone to a real school instead of Miss Grossmont's Academy of Secretarial Arts in Missoula."

Jordan scratched his head. "I'm still waiting for the part where you tell me how you became Camilla's silent partner."

Mac straightened to her full height of five feet. "I may have started out as a secretary with a pretty face, sport, but I've learned a little bit about how businesses work while I've been with Taylor Beef. Got a bonus every year, including those years during the recession when Cornelius the Second had to make massive cuts. He gave me stock in the company and it turns out I'm pretty good at knowing a great investment when I see it."

"Well, Camilla is certainly the best investment around." Jordan smiled at his new fiancée. Man, he wouldn't get tired of calling her that. Actually, he couldn't wait to start calling her his wife.

"My assistant dean asked me to come speak in one of her intro classes the week after you and I were there. When Mac saw me on campus with my Integrated Project proposal, she seemed really interested. I told her how I'd gone to the Denim and Diamonds gala hoping to meet a few potential investors. She suggested that was a waste of my time."

"Not a complete waste, I hope." Jordan smirked. "After all, that's where you met me."

Mac chuckled. "I believe my exact words were, why go after prince charming when everyone knows it's the fairy godmothers who get things done?"

Jordan leaned over the counter to wrap the older woman in a tight hug. "Mac, I should've known. I couldn't imagine a better fairy godmother than you."

The older woman wiped something from below her eye before she straightened her ball cap. "Speaking of getting things done, sport, you need to move along and let me go back to work before this hot cocoa line gets out of control."

Jordan grabbed his drink off the table, winked at a clearly flustered Mac, then threw his arm across Camilla's shoulders as they walked along the park.

"So, you don't mind that Mac and I will be working together?" Camilla asked as she looked up at him, her knit cap causing her brown hair to burst out in a riot of curls around her face.

"Are you kidding? Mac is barely in the office as it is. It'll be good for her to have a whole other reason to sneak out of work for something that isn't baseball related."

"Well, she'll still be getting her sports fix.

One of her conditions was that I agree to have big-screen TVs in the bar area."

Jordan slapped his hand to his forehead right as Camilla leaned into him, throwing them both off balance. He recovered quickly, but not before he bumped into a man staring down at his smart phone.

"Sorry about that," he told the man, but the guy seemed to be lost in whatever he was reading on his screen.

As they continued through the park, more people offered their congratulations. Every time Camilla smiled or waved at someone, Jordan's heart stretched and his chest filled with pride. When she paused in front of the giant Christmas tree to stare at the bright star on top, he stood behind her, wrapping his arms around her waist and drawing her against him. She sighed and leaned the back of her head against his shoulder.

He kissed her temple. "It's only the beginning of December, and so far this Christmas is promising to be the best one yet."

She turned in his arms. "But I haven't even given you your gift yet."

"You said yes," he told her. "That's the only gift I need."

Epilogue

Desperately Seeking Daisy

Desperately seeking a woman named Daisy who was born in 1945 to teenage parents and placed for adoption somewhere in Montana. Your birth family would like to meet you! Please contact the Abernathy family at the Ambling A Ranch, Bronco Heights, Montana. Time is of the essence!

The man's eyes widened as he read the social media notice on his phone.

He looked around, as if to make sure no one

had seen his reaction to the post. The couple who'd bumped into him a few seconds ago only had eyes for each other. Most of the other revelers were either in lines for food or still gathered around the newly lit Christmas tree in front of Bronco City Hall. Between all the noise from the carolers singing up on the stage and the kids racing by to take their sleds to the plowed slope behind his vendor booth, the man was surrounded by yuletide overload.

Bah humbug! he thought. There was no way he would've attended the small town's annual event if his local business didn't require it.

He certainly wouldn't have been scrolling through his phone if he wasn't completely bored by all the festivities. Which meant he never would have seen the online notice. It probably was just a coincidence.

There was no reason for him to worry. No sense in stirring up trouble.

* * * * *

Look for A Cowboy's Christmas Carol
by Brenda Harlen
the next book in the new
Harlequin Special Edition continuity
Montana Mavericks: What Happened to Beatrix?
On sale December 2020, wherever
Harlequin books and ebooks are sold.

And catch up with the previous
Montana Mavericks titles:

In Search of the Long-Lost Maverick
by New York Times *bestselling author*
Christine Rimmer

The Cowboy's Comeback
by Melissa Senate

The Maverick's Baby Arrangement
by Kathy Douglass

The Cowboy's Promise
by Teresa Southwick

His Christmas Cinderella
by Christy Jeffries

Available now!

**WE HOPE YOU ENJOYED
THIS BOOK FROM**

Believe in love. Overcome obstacles. Find happiness.

Relate to finding comfort and strength in the
support of loved ones and enjoy the journey
no matter what life throws your way.

6 NEW BOOKS AVAILABLE EVERY MONTH!

#2803 A COWBOY'S CHRISTMAS CAROL
Montana Mavericks: What Happened to Beatrix?
by Brenda Harlen

Evan Cruise is haunted by his past and refuses to celebrate the festivities around him—until he meets Daphne Taylor. But when Daphne uncovers Evan's shocking family secret, it threatens to tear them apart. Will a little Christmas magic change everything?

#2804 A TEMPORARY CHRISTMAS ARRANGEMENT
The Bravos of Valentine Bay • by Christine Rimmer

Neither Harper Bravo nor Lincoln Stryker is planning to stay in Valentine Bay. But when Lincoln moves in next door and needs a hand with his nice and nephew, cash-strapped Harper can't help but step in. They make a deal: just during the holiday season, she'll nanny the kids while he works. But will love be enough to have them both changing their plans?

#2805 HIS LAST-CHANCE CHRISTMAS FAMILY
Welcome to Starlight • by Michelle Major

Brynn Hale has finally returned home to Starlight. She's ready for a fresh start for her son, and what better time for it than Christmas? Still, Nick Dunlap is the one connection to her past she can't let go of. Nick's not sure he deserves a chance with her now, but the magic of the season might make forgiveness—and love—a little bit easier for them both...

#2806 FOR THIS CHRISTMAS ONLY
Masterson, Texas • by Caro Carson

A chance encounter at the town's Yule log lighting leads Eli Taylor to invite Mallory Ames to stay with him. Which turns into asking her to be his fake girlfriend to show his siblings what a genuinely loving partnership looks like...just while they visit for the holidays. But will their lesson turn into something real for both of them?

#2807 A FIREHOUSE CHRISTMAS BABY
Lovestruck, Vermont • by Teri Wilson

After her dreams of motherhood were dashed, Felicity Hart is determined to make a fresh start in Lovestruck. Unfortunately, she has to work with firefighter Wade Ericson when a baby is abandoned at the firehouse. Then Felicity finds herself moving into Wade's house and using her foster-care training to care for the child, all just in time for Christmas.

#2808 A SOLDIER UNDER HER TREE
Sweet Briar Sweethearts • by Kathy Douglass

When her ex-fiancé shows up at her shop—engaged to her sister!—dress designer Hannah Carpenter doesn't know what to do. Especially when former fling Russell Danielson rides to the rescue, offering a fake relationship to foil her rude relations. The thing is, there's nothing fake about his kiss...

SPECIAL EXCERPT FROM

♦ HARLEQUIN
SPECIAL EDITION

*Brynn Hale, single mom widowed after an unhappy
marriage, has finally returned home to Starlight.
She's ready for a fresh start for her son, and what
better time for it than Christmas? But Nick Dunlap is
the one connection to her past she can't let go of...*

*Read on for a sneak peek at the next book in the
Welcome to Starlight miniseries,*
His Last-Chance Christmas Family
by Michelle Major.

"You sound like a counselor." The barest glimmer of
a smile played around the edges of Brynn's mouth.
"When did you get so smart, Chief Dunlap?"

"I was born this way. You never noticed before now
because you were too dazzled by my good looks."

Her eyes went wide for a moment, and he wondered
if he'd overstepped with the teasing. "I was dazzled
by you. That part is true." She rolled her eyes. "But I
guarantee you didn't show this kind of insight when we
were younger."

He should make some funny comment back to her,
keep the moment light. Instead, he let his gaze lower to
her mouth as he took the soft ends of her hair between

his fingers. "I might not have messed things up so badly if I had."

She drew in a sharp breath and he stepped away. This was not the time to spook her. "Come on, Brynn," he coaxed. "We both know it's not going to be good for anyone if you stay with your mom."

"She doesn't even want to meet Remi," Brynn told him, her full lips pressing into a thin line.

"Her loss," he said quietly. "All along it's been her loss. Say yes. Please."

She shifted and looked to where Tyler had disappeared with Kel. Without turning back to Nick, she nodded. "Yes," she said finally. "Thank you for the offer. I appreciate it and promise we won't disrupt your life." Now she did turn to him. "Very much, anyway," she added with a smile.

"Easy as pie," he said, ignoring the fact that his heart was beating as fast as if he'd just finished running a marathon.

Don't miss
His Last-Chance Christmas Family *by Michelle Major,*
available December 2020 wherever
Harlequin Special Edition books and ebooks are sold.

Harlequin.com